Escape fr

For thrills and adventure
readers everywhere love
Peter Lerangis

ANTARCTICA

Journey to the Pole
Escape from Disaster

WATCHERS

#1 LAST STOP
#2 REWIND
#3 I.D.
#4 WAR
#5 ISLAND
#6 LAB 6

ANTARCTICA

Escape from Disaster

Peter Lerangis

AN
APPLE
PAPERBACK

SCHOLASTIC INC.
New York Toronto London Auckland Sydney
Mexico City New Delhi Hong Kong

No part of this work may be reproduced in whole or in part, or stored in a retrieval system, or transmitted in any form or by any means, electronic, mechanical, photocopying, recording, or otherwise, without written permission of the publisher. For information regarding permission, write to Scholastic Inc., Attention: Permissions Department, 555 Broadway, New York, NY 10012.

ISBN 0-439-16388-9

Copyright © 2000 by Peter Lerangis.
All rights reserved. Published by Scholastic Inc.
SCHOLASTIC and associated logos are trademarks and/or registered trademarks of Scholastic Inc.

12 11 10 9 8 7 6 5 4 3 2   0 1 2 3 4 5/0

Printed in the U.S.A.   40
First Scholastic printing, July 2000

For David Levithan

Antarctica as it was in 1909.

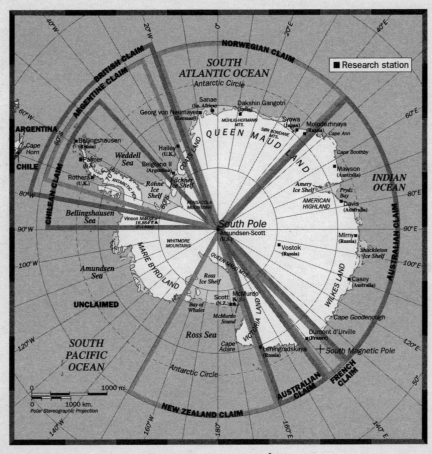

Antarctica as it is today.

Crew and company of the *Mystery*, as of January 10, 1910:

Jack Winslow — expedition leader

Elias Barth — captain

Peter Mansfield — second in command and chief navigator

Colin Winslow — third in command

John Siegal — first mate

Luis Rivera — second mate

Andrew Douglas Winslow — junior officer

Dr. Ross Montfort — general physician

Dr. Harold Riesman — veterinarian

Dr. Frank Nesbit — biologist

Harv Talmadge — meteorologist

Jacques Petard — physical instructor and chaplain

David Ruskey — photographer

Kosta Kontonikolaos — dog handler

Sam Bailey, Pete Hayes, Vincent Lombardo, Mike Sanders, Chris Ruppenthal, Bruce Cranston, George Oppenheim, James Windham, Robert (last name unknown) — able seamen

Tim O'Malley — able seaman/second cook

Hank Brillman — electrician

Wyman Kennedy — carpenter

Horst Flummerfelt — machinist

Rick Stimson — cook

Philip Westfall — helpmeet at large

Nigel (last name unknown) — stowaway

Chionni, Demosthenes, Dimitriou, Eleni, Fotis, Iosif, Ireni, Kalliope, Kristina, Maria, Martha, Megalamatia, Michalaki, Nikola, Panagiotis, Pericles, Plutarchos, Socrates, Sounion, Stavros, Yiorgos, Zeus — dogs

Deceased:

Dr. David Shreve — geologist (*fell into crevasse, November 20, 1909, during sledge journey toward South Pole*)

Thirteen dogs: *Aspros, Galactobouriko, Hera, Hercules, Kukla, Loukoumada, Plato, Skylaki, Taki, Taso* (with *Shreve*); *Tsitsifies, Vrechi, Yanni* (of dysentery)

Part One

Trapped

1

Andrew

Journal of A. D. Winslow · 1ˢᵗ entry — 10 Jan, 1910

Ross Sea, Antarctica

Back aboard <u>Mystery</u>. Fingers & face frstbittn. Hurts to write. Have exposure. Recovering n bed. Ship iced in. Crew trying to get hr out. Will be here a while. May as well strt this j.nal.

Failed to reach S. Pole. Team is 9 days back. Left 14 Nov. Lost food/supplies in avalnche. Dr. Shreve dead — crevasse. 13 dogs dead. Lombardo weak — heart attck. Kosta (dog handler) — toes amputated. Oppenheim mentally unstable. Almost didn't make it myself. Colin dug me out of a snowbank & saved my life.

While we went, 1/2 of <u>Mystery</u> crew stayed here. Nigel & Philip led mutiny w/8 men — wanted to sail home w/out us. Colin stopped them, put them in brig. Capt. Barth made Colin 3rd in command.
Colin is

Andrew put down his pencil. Blood oozed from the broken, coal-black skin on his index finger and dripped onto the page. He lay back and let the notebook fall open on his chest. The cut throbbed, sharp and unrelenting. All his sores did — on his hands, wrists, face, feet.

The *Mystery*'s afterhold had become a makeshift hospital. The entire South Pole crew had required treatment upon returning, but now only Kosta, Lombardo, Oppenheim, and Andrew remained belowdecks.

Outside, the crew pounded on the ice that trapped the ship. Captain Barth's voice was clear through four feet of hull: *"Put your weight into it, men!"*

Andrew wanted to rise up and help — step outside, grip an ax in his frostbitten palms, and hack with the best of them. He was different now. The trip across the continent had changed him. He wasn't the kid they thought he was: the expedition leader's stepson. A dreamer. A bookworm. A sixteen-year-old landlubber playing sailor.

But he couldn't very well prove it in the afterhold.

Andrew had learned the unspoken lessons of the sailors. Every day was a battle — position and planning, strategy and tactics. Life was about survival. Using the enemy's strength to your advantage. Trimming your sails against a strong head wind, lowering them before a storm. Finding shelter under a pressure ridge and warmth in a cave of solid ice. Learning never to repeat your mistakes.

Andrew had fought his battle and lost. He had collapsed leading a dog sledge across the continent, with no reliable navigation and a partner who could neither speak English nor walk.

The sledge had traveled onward without him, 200 yards before reaching the *Mystery*. If his stepbrother, Colin, hadn't found him, Andrew would have frozen, his body preserved forever in an ice cap that would push northward and eventually send him, encased in an iceberg, out to sea.

Andrew was grateful to Colin. Everyone was.

Colin had foiled Nigel and Philip's mutiny. The crew respected Colin. *We knew he had it in him*, they all said; *he was just waiting for the right opportunity*.

But they weren't saying that before November.

Colin had been a thorn in everyone's side, surly and lazy. He'd been against this trip from the beginning. He felt it was wrong to leave New York so soon after his stepmother had died. It showed that Jack was obsessed and coldhearted.

But Colin hadn't seen the truth, as Andrew had. Mother would have said *go*. Better to roll up your sleeves and follow your dream instead of moping while it faded away.

But what happened when you followed the dream and failed — when a glorious quest ended in mishaps, bad judgment, death, and disaster?

You bled. Your body suffered hypothermia and starvation. You were bedridden with the lame, the weak, and the crazy. You had everyone's sympathy.

You didn't have respect.

Andrew swung his legs around. The mission may have failed, but he would get the respect he deserved. He wouldn't let them treat him as if he were a child. A *child* couldn't revive an entire expedition when its members had nearly frozen to death in a cave. A child didn't save the life of a man determined to die, the way Andrew had when Kosta insisted he be left to freeze with his dogs.

A child didn't sit and stew when there was work to be done.

Holding tight to the wooden bunk frame, Andrew eased himself off the bedding. The last time he'd tried to walk, three days ago, he couldn't support his own weight.

His feet hit the deck solidly. Slowly he released his fingers from the frame. His knees did not buckle. He walked in a circle, testing his leg muscles. Painful, but not excruciating. He felt a little dizzy, but that was to be expected. His belly, around which he'd had to cinch his trouser waist with a rope, now felt a bit flabby, if that was possible.

His ankles still had open sores, and his hands and face stung. But cuts didn't kill. Quickly he put on three pairs of socks, then slipped on his boots, parka, and hat. He wrapped clean bandages around his hands before putting on gloves.

"*Andreou, filos mou,*" Kosta said, "*pou pas?*"

Andrew recognized that expression. *Where are you going?*

"*Epàno,*" Andrew replied. *Up.*

"*Etsi bravo!*" Kosta cheered Andrew's vocabulary but his expression instantly turned to dismay, and he protested in a rapid staccato of words that Andrew neither understood nor obeyed as he climbed abovedecks.

The sunlight's glare hurt more than the cold.

Andrew pulled a pair of goggles from his pocket and put them on. The straps felt like metal files.

The ship's dogs scampered outside their kennels, which lined both port and starboard sides, crowding the deck. There were only twenty-two of the original thirty-five; six had been lost on the journey to the South Pole, seven more on the retreat. The survivors were beginning to gain weight now, and as Andrew hobbled across the deck they fought over penguin pemmican and scraps of seal meat.

He cautiously climbed onto one of the port kennels, then hoisted his legs over the gunwale.

The scene was worse than he'd expected. Ice surrounded the *Mystery* on all sides. Two floes had converged on her, one pushing at port, the other at starboard. The term for this was *pressure*, which was like calling dynamite a candle. This kind of thing happened all the time in Antarctica. With nowhere to go, two colliding ice floes would shove each other's edges upward, groaning like a wounded sea god. Eventually one side would win, pushing over the top of the other, smashing the tented ice into a broken, mountainous heap, a *pressure ridge*.

Andrew could see that the port-side floe was

pushing on the ship, the starboard-side floe was pushing down.

The *Mystery* itself was a pressure ridge.

Colin and Jack hacked at the ice around the prow. Mansfield, the second in command, pulled a giant saw through the ice that encroached on the port hull. Even the prisoners had been let out to help — which made sense, since escape was hardly a danger. Nigel, the stowaway who had led the mutiny, was using a mallet, striking a wedged chisel with insane fury, trying to dislodge the ice.

As Andrew slowly made his way down the gangplank, the men were too obsessed to notice him — except Philip Westfall.

"Well. The return of the prodigal son." Philip leaned on a large shovel. He was bundled in a thick overcoat covered with a canvas tarpaulin. The dry pallor of his face contrasted starkly with the sweaty ruddiness of the men around him.

"Are you using that shovel, Philip?" Andrew asked.

"Does it look as if I am?" Philip said. "Of course I am. It is my prop. It keeps me from lying down, a condition I desire madly but dare not assume, under penalty of death, no doubt."

The brig hadn't changed Philip. He had fit in among the crew about as well as a poodle among oxen — a seventeen-year-old rich boy who had tried to pass himself off as a twenty-one-year-old sailor. He was on the voyage only because he was the nephew of Horace Putney.

Putney had financed the entire expedition. He was stinking rich (less polite people would leave out the word "rich"). Jack would never say exactly how Putney had made his money, which meant it couldn't have been legal. But when none of Jack's wealthy old Harvard pals would commit a dime toward the undertaking, Jack went to Putney, and Putney ponied up. All he wanted in return was a share of the glory after the ship arrived home — and to be rid of his nephew, whom his sister had sent from London to live with him.

"I don't suppose I can use your prop to do a little work?" Andrew asked.

Philip handed it over. "As long as you promise to agree when I claim that you wrenched it from my grasp against my will."

Andrew took the shovel and walked toward the *Mystery*'s hull. Out of the corner of his eye he saw Colin staring at him. Andrew smiled weakly.

A group of men had managed to drive a crack

in the ice parallel to the hull. Captain Barth was among them. He looked warily at Andrew. "You know, you don't have to do this, Winslow."

"I want to," Andrew said.

Barth grunted approvingly. "We're making good progress. Should break through by the end of the day. Stay on this side and help. Gravity will help pull her down and that'll wrench up the starboard side and bust her loose."

Andrew looked toward the horizon for streams that led through the ice. "Any leads?"

"There's a water sky north-by-northwest. Ruskey reported seeing some leads before it, about half a mile away. I have a team clearing the prow. When we're in the clear, we'll charge up the engine and use the hull as a battering ram through the ice. If the wind holds from the south, it may blow the pack out to sea, and we're home free. But if it shifts . . ."

Barth let his words trail off, but Andrew knew what he meant. The pack, thousands of sheets of floating ice, was trapped in a sea surrounded on three sides by land. A north wind would push the ice south, jamming it into the Antarctic coast. The leads would close up fast, trapping the *Mystery* again.

And the wind was changing. Andrew felt it.

As Barth moved away, Andrew slammed his

shovel into the crack. It opened a few more inches to the left.

He slammed again and again.

"Attaboy," someone called, but Andrew wasn't paying attention. His whole body was working now. The pain was forgotten, and he felt exhilarated. He was hitting just as hard as they were. Harder.

Thrust.

With each smack of the shovel blade, more water peeked through from below.

Thrust.

It wouldn't be long now. They were going to make it.

Thrust.

Thrust.

Thrust.

On a backstroke the shovel flew out of his hands into the air. Andrew stumbled forward, smashing into the hull.

"Look out!" someone yelled.

The men scattered. The shovel thumped to the ice, narrowly missing Pete Hayes.

Colin ran over to Andrew. "Are you all right?"

Andrew sat, his back against the ship, catching his breath. He had done too much, too fast. "I'm — fine."

"You have to pace yourself, Andrew."

"I know . . . I know. Sorry."

"When you're tired and worn out and sick, things like that happen."

"I'm not sick anymore. I'm trying to help, Colin. You need me out here. You need all the help you can get —"

"*Help* is the word, yes. *Help*. If you're able to provide it, then do the work. If not, then give that shovel to someone who can."

"Well spoken," Philip said, briskly marching forward. With a flourish, he scooped the shovel off the ice, then jammed it into the crack. "Take *that*!"

The ship moved.

All work stopped. One by one, the men dropped their shovels.

"What did I do?" Philip murmured.

"Step back!" Captain Barth shouted. "Now!"

The men turned and ran. Colin pulled Andrew by the arm.

Slowly the massive hull lurched downward. It settled heavily in the sea, sending up a swell that flooded water onto the ice, pushing the tools away from the ship.

A cheer broke out from the starboard side.

The *Mystery* was out of its trap.

"I don't believe this," Andrew said.

Philip stared at his shovel. "Neither do I."

"Flummerfelt, get to the engine room!" Barth shouted.

"Next port of call, Argentina!" Rivera hooted.

"Home of the best steaks in the world!" O'Malley added, dancing an impromptu jig.

Finally. This was it. The last leg. Buenos Aires and then New York City. Home.

Andrew could feel the sights and sounds of Bond Street — its soot-choked air, its paving stones befouled with horse dung, its constant clamor of passing vagrants and machine noise. It had never seemed more exotic and welcoming.

Jack called out over the din: "Keep hacking, men — we're not free yet!"

As the water receded, the crewmen scrambled for their picks and axes.

Andrew ran for his shovel. His ankles were killing him now. As he grabbed the handle, the sores on his hands shot pain through his body. He dropped the shovel and let out a yowl.

"Someone grab that shovel!" Barth called out.

A deep moan, like the blast of a trombone, rose up from within the *Mystery*.

The hull lurched again, but this time toward

the men, closing the gap between them and the ship. It jammed against the edge of the ice floe.

CRRACK!

At the sound of splitting timber from the other side of the ship, the crew ran around to starboard.

The center of the starboard hull was cracked, penetrated by a giant column of ice.

2

Colin

January 10, 1910

"She's stove in," Andrew murmured.

"We can *see* that," Colin said.

"Translation of *stove in?*" Philip asked.

"Cracked open," said Nigel. "Like your head'll be if you keep asking stupid questions."

"We may have helped the starboard-side floe by relieving port-side pressure," Jack said.

Colin struck at the ice column. The other men joined him with renewed force.

Nigel was at his right. "We'll never cut frew this!"

"Oh, it's a big boat," Philip said as he pounded with his shovel. "It'll survive."

"*Ship*, you block'ead, not *boat*," Nigel snapped. "And it's a *she*."

"It's made of *wood*," Philip said. "Wood cannot be female."

"You inherited yer brain from yer pa's side, then?"

"Nigel, run along and start a mutiny amongst the penguins —"

"*Will you knock it off and get to work?*" Colin shouted.

The ice was tilted upward at a forty-five-degree angle. It had bent the wooden planking enough to push through the outer layer.

The planks were made of greenheart. Greenheart was like steel, Father had said. And with two feet of solid oak and Norwegian mountain fir behind it, the hull was supposed to be indestructible.

But wood was wood. Under enough pressure greenheart splintered, too.

"*Harder! Harder!*" Colin yelled, bringing his pick down sharply, sending hunks of ice hurling into the air.

"Hey, John Henry, put down that hammer," drawled Wyman Kennedy's voice. "You 'n' me's got a job to do."

Kennedy was the ship's carpenter, a North Carolinian with a sense of humor so sharp you could scrape paint with it. He was standing behind Colin with Captain Barth and the ship's machinist, Horst Flummerfelt.

"The hole's beneath the waterline," Barth explained. "When the ice gives way, the water'll pour in."

"Your pops wants you to help me find some wood and build us a cofferdam to seal off the hull," Kennedy said. "Let's go."

Colin followed Kennedy to the gangplank. They scrambled up the side and over. From the deckhouse, Kennedy began pulling out planks of wood. "It's got to be watertight," he said. "No cuttin' corners."

Kennedy worked fast and talked fast. They nailed planks together, fitted joints, reinforced corners. When the contraption was done, Kennedy began drawing curved diagonal lines down the sides of the walls. "Cut along here, so we can fit the thing to the hull."

"Aren't you going to measure the angle against the hull?" Colin asked.

"Don't need to," Kennedy said. "A good doctor knows his patients."

CRRRRRRACK!

The sound was like a cannon shot. The ship jolted sideways. Colin fell to the deck.

"*Evacuate ship!*" Father's voice cried out. "*Get Lombardo, Kosta, and Oppenheim out of there!*"

"Aye, aye!" Colin scrambled to his feet. Racing ahead of Kennedy, he went down into the afterhold.

Kosta was on the floor, grimacing with pain, his cane lying next to him. "*Pos épatheh?*"

"*Ella!*" Colin said. It was one of the few Greek words he knew. *Come.*

He helped Kosta up. As they walked haltingly back to the ladder, Kennedy tried to lift the snoring Lombardo.

Oppenheim, still rocking, let out an explosive cackle. "He sleeps. Yeah, verily, he sleeps while the kingdom burns."

"Oppenheim, follow us!" Colin commanded. "You're the only healthy one here."

Sort of, he thought.

He and Kosta emerged abovedecks into the sun. Robert, the African expatriate they'd picked up in Buenos Aires, reached toward Kosta and lifted him as if he were a basket of fruit, then gently lowered him over the gunwale, into the arms of waiting crewmen.

Colin turned and helped Lombardo up the ladder. Oppenheim took a little more prodding.

When the ship was clear, Jack quickly divided the men into three teams. "Mansfield, your men stay here and keep at the ice. Rivera, you're salvage. Your team unloads all four lifeboats, then grabs whatever it can — spare masts, sails and spars, cofferdam, mess and carpentry equipment, wood, rope, and canvas — just drop it in the snow. Move fast and be ready to bolt if Captain Barth or I give the signal to evacuate. Colin, you get a team to find the tents and cots and set up camp. We'll stay out here until the pack blows out. Now, *go!*"

Within minutes, Colin's team had unloaded supplies and was hammering stakes in the ice. Robert and Brillman designed new tents on the fly, stretching sailcloth and canvas over two-by-fours because the real tents had been lost by Andrew and his expedition.

Andrew struggled to help out, but he couldn't lift anything without wincing.

"The infirmary tent first," Colin commanded. "Three cots."

"Two," Andrew said. "I don't need one."

"Just in case."

"The worst is behind me, Colin."

"It's not always about you. Three cots. In case of emergencies."

The men set to work and finished the cots quickly, two of them especially wide — for Lombardo's girth and for Kosta's habit of curling up with his dogs.

Father poked his head through the tent flap. "Good job on the camp, fellas. What'll we call it?"

"Camp . . . Ice!" Flummerfelt suggested eagerly. "'Cause of all the ice."

"Brilliant," murmured Sam Bailey.

"Death Valley," Oppenheim said.

"Camp Perseverance," Andrew suggested.

Father smiled. "Like it, Andrew! You've always had a way with words."

"Thanks, Pop."

Colin set to tightening the lines. He couldn't bear to look at Andrew's smug little face.

Ease up, Colin told himself. Andrew had been through enough. He'd almost died in the snow.

He deserved compassion and sympathy.

So why, in the middle of this mess, was it so easy to *hate* him?

Because Andrew was so *good,* that was why. Good at words, at mathematics, at pleasing people. He had read everything and could talk rings around

21

Colin. And why not? He'd grown up with books on his shelves and time on his hands, Andrew Douglas of Beacon Hill in his big brick house near the Boston Common, surrounded by the swells of high society.

He hadn't grown up worrying whether there'd be enough heat to last the Alaskan winter. Whether Mother would return from her Arctic journeys.

Whether life was possible after she *didn't* return. After the sea took her.

Being an Anglo, Father could pack up and return to *his* land. But Colin would always be away from home. Running from painful reminders of her. Never fitting in.

Here in Antarctica he was surrounded by reminders — the sky and the snow and the constant summer sun and the icy waters.

Clever Andrew could never know that.

Colin left the tent. Outside, O'Malley had set up two stoves and was cooking some blubbery meat with Stimson. Rivera and his crew were dumping enormous piles of rigging and spare wood over the *Mystery*'s stern bulwark, far from the feverish chopping of Mansfield and his team. The hole was now clear of ice, but the ridge was still thick, pressing hard against the lower part of the hull. Kennedy and

Flummerfelt had taken up work on the cofferdam once again.

It was an act of great optimism, Colin thought.

Father was helping drag Rivera's pile away from the ship. Colin ran over to help, grabbing one end of a thick column of polished oak, no doubt a spare mizzenmast.

Captain Barth approached from the bow, his face grim and furrowed. "We're going to have to divert men to starboard," he said. "The pack is blowing in. It's encroaching again on the other side. The gap's our only hope, and it's just about closed —"

GRRRRROMMM!

Mansfield jumped away from the hull.

Kennedy and Flummerfelt stopped work on the cofferdam.

Colin felt his stomach twist. He looked up toward the source of the noise.

The *Mystery*'s foremast wasn't in its usual place. Not quite. Its crosstrees were angled to starboard, as if it were turning to take a peek at the horizon.

"God save us," Captain Barth muttered.

"GET THE MEN OUT OF THERE!" Father shouted. "NOW!"

3

Philip

January 10, 1910

The money. All that mattered was the money.

Philip draped two coats on his bedding and looked behind him.

Ruskey was the only other person in the after-hold, but his back was firmly turned.

Philip reached into his footlocker, grabbed bills by the fistful, and began stuffing pockets. First the overcoat. Then the pea coat. Then the tweed jacket he was wearing. From outside to in. When finished, he would don them all.

No one would notice the thickness of three coats. In their winter clothing, the men were all the size of thatched huts anyway — and if the *Mys-*

tery sank, a chest filled with English pound notes would do little good floating beneath the Antarctic Ocean. Indigestion for the seals, perhaps. Hardly a hospitable thing to do to one's hosts.

Besides, Philip had a responsibility. The money belonged to the Bank of London. Yes, he'd stolen it (although he'd swear he'd been tricked into it), and no, he had no intention of returning it. But the money was created by hardworking Britons who meant it to be *used*, not wasted. Giving it up was positively unpatriotic.

The noise upstairs — abovedecks, or whatever grammatical monstrosity they called it — was grotesque. No doubt some mizzen or binnacle or barnacle had broken loose. The men were all afraid the ship would collapse. Nonsense. The hole was small and the hull was thicker than a London fog.

He hated the atmosphere out there. Chop, chop, chop, all day long, until your hands resembled bangers and mash. And for what? Why not leave the poor ice floes alone, let them mix it up and get it out of their systems? That would be the sensible approach.

The next best thing was to remain here as long as possible.

"Westfall?"

Philip slammed the chest shut. "*What?* I mean . . . yes, David?"

Ruskey was kneeling by an old wooden crate. He was poring over his photographic plates, holding them up to the light, dropping some into the crate and discarding others on the deck. "Do you think this really captures the aurora australis, or would you go for this shot of the ice shelf?"

"Well . . . uh . . ."

Lord, how was he to distinguish one of those black filmy things from another?

Philip was responsible for those photographs. Uncle Horace had made that clear. They were the entire reason for his financing the trip. *You can't make money on glory,* he'd said. *But a five-cent reproducible image'll make you rich beyond your wildest dreams.* Uncle Horace had joked that he would release Philip's whereabouts to the British authorities if Philip failed to retain the film.

Uncle Horace was not a joking man.

And Philip was no fool.

The more Ruskey packed, the better. And by the by, if one or two images just *happened* to end up in Philip's possession, well, no one would be the worse off for it.

"I'd say just pack them all," Philip advised.

"Can't," Ruskey replied. "I have to weld them into metal containers to waterproof them. Captain Barth will allow only twenty containers. I'll take my Vest-Pocket Kodak. It takes lousy pictures, but —"

"*Twenty?* Balderdash. The man has no appreciation of art!"

"This is about weight, not art. If we travel by sledge, we have to keep it light. I learned that the hard way on our South Pole trip."

"Yes, but we're heading *north*, where it's warmer!"

Footsteps clomped upward from steerage, and Nigel emerged with a bag filled with food. "Anchoo foonfeh yut?"

"Swallow, please?" Philip said.

Nigel gulped hard, then belched. From all indications, he had eaten sardines and chocolate for lunch.

"Ain't you *finished* yet?" he asked, winking furiously.

"Almost."

Wink wink wink wink. "I trust you ain't forget-tin' to take all yer *valuables*, if you catch me drift-wood."

"Yes, Nigel."

Lovely. All the subtlety of a whale among gold-fish.

Nigel was a fool. A blinking idiot. What kind of man stowed away on a ship to *Antarctica*, for heaven's sake? The same kind of man who would organize a mutiny on a ship locked in ice, that's who. A British man.

On that October day Philip discovered Nigel in steerage, he should have smitten him with a whale bone. But no, Philip was kind, Philip chose mercy — and his reward? The lout had *recognized* Philip from the newspaper, from that hideous photo they'd printed under the headline LONDON SCHOOL-BOY THEFT. To buy Nigel's silence, Philip took the blame for smuggling him on board. Nigel, the story went, was Philip's friend.

The fact that the crew believed him was the greatest insult of all.

One little scandal and you paid for months. The entire arrangement was unfair.

Suddenly Colin Winslow's voice honked from the hatch:

"EVACUATE SHIP! THE FOREMAST IS BREAKING!"

"Well, fix it," Philip said under his breath.

Ruskey grabbed his camera. "*This* I have to see."

Pulling along his wooden chest, Ruskey headed for the hatch. He left behind an enormous pile of discarded plates — no doubt glorious Antarctic panoramas for which Americans would pay dearly to hang in gilded frames over their fireplaces.

They simply couldn't be left here.

Philip grabbed six. Six would do. He could easily pack them away without anyone knowing. Once the ship returned, he could move to Chicago under an assumed name and sell them on the black market.

But where to hide them? He glanced around and saw a large half-filled burlap sack marked HARD-TACK. Nigel must have dropped it on the way out. Perfect. Hardtack tasted like cardboard and no one in his right mind would bother opening the bag.

SREEEEEEEEE!

The blasted whistle again.

"ALL MEN MOVE AWAY FROM THE SHIP!" Captain Barth thundered.

"Yes, yes, hold your sea horses. . . ." Philip jammed the photos into the sack. They stuck out the top. He reached into the bottom of the bag and shifted around the stale, wretched biscuits to make more room.

Now for the bills. He'd wasted so much precious time on this, he'd left the coats on the bed — and the bulk of the money still in the trunk.

He stood up, lifted the bag, and lost his balance.

It moved. The ship *jumped*.

Had it — *she* — already shaken free of the ice?

A deep sound moaned from above him — and Philip knew in an instant, in his gut, that he had to leave.

He heard the crash a split second before the deck exploded.

4

Jack

January 10, 1910

Foremast: smashed the deck. Propped up by the engine room bulkhead. Needs replacement, not repair.

Main: still standing but cracked. Replacement, but the wood could be salvaged for good use.

Deck: repair needs at least half the rescued planking.

Ship: evacuated.

Crew: on the ice. Count them off . . . one . . . two . . . three . . .

It helped to think clearly. Avoid panic. Assess the situation, ask questions. All exploration, all human nature boiled down to one thing — finding the right questions to ask.

Could she make it? Impossible to know. The damage was severe, yes. But two masts and a stove-in hull did not a ship make. She was still the *Mystery*, and if any ship could hold, she could.

Eleven . . . twelve . . . thirteen . . . fourteen . . .

Positive thinking. Shackleton made it back under worse circumstances. Nansen would let his ship ice up on purpose — just like this. He knew the moving floe would move the ship. He made a technique of it.

Twenty-one . . . twenty-two . . . twenty-three . . .

The men weren't panicking. That was good. They were a plucky bunch. Nerves of steel. Swarming around, all business, doing the work that needed to be —

Twenty-nine.

One short.

There should have been thirty.

Colin-Andrew-Barth-Kennedy-Hayes-Robert-Rivera-Flummerfelt-Cranston-O'Malley-Talmadge-Petard-Bailey-Nigel —

"Nigel, where's Philip?" Jack blurted out.

"Who cares?" muttered Ruppenthal.

Nigel shrugged. "I fought 'e came out."

"He did," Ruskey agreed. "He followed me out of the afterhold."

"Then, where is he?" Jack asked. "Is he in any of the tents? Colin?"

Colin shook his head.

"Did anyone actually *see* him climb up that ladder?"

Ruskey's face went blank.

"'E *better*'a come out," Nigel said, looking suddenly pale.

Not another crew member. Not right under his nose.

Jack sprinted to the *Mystery* and up the gangplank. The deck was destroyed. The mast lay across it like a fallen larch, its base still tenuously attached, its crosstrees akimbo. Its top rested heavily on the engine casing, just below the surface of the deck. It hadn't fallen all the way through. Yet.

"Philip!"

No answer.

Jack jumped down into an afterhold that was unrecognizable — the deck covered with splinters and shattered planks, the air thick with sawdust and snow. *"Philip, are you down here?"*

"Oh . . . oh, dear . . ."

Under the mast.

Jack dropped to the deck and saw a bare foot jutting out of a pile of wood. In the shadow of the foremast an arm moved. "I . . . seem to be having a bit of . . . difficulty."

"Hold on, Philip!" Jack cleared away planks of heavy wood. "Do you think you can walk?"

Philip was sitting up now, dazed and ashen-faced. "I — I believe I'm all right."

"Grab my arm!"

"My — my coats — they're on my bunk —"

"The bunk is destroyed!"

"It — it can't be. I must get those coats —"

"Philip, the mast isn't stable. The ship's in trouble. Let's go!"

He reached out, but Philip pulled away. "I also had a bag. It's filled with . . . hardtack."

"There's no time for that, Philip —"

"Here it is!" Philip pulled a burlap sack from under a pile. Directly over his head the foremast twisted, grinding against the steel engine.

Jack lunged for the boy's arm. Philip jumped away.

With a sharp report, the column snapped. Jack scrambled to get out of the way.

Too late. A broken spar slammed against his thigh, pinning him to the floor.

He breathed wood. He choked on wood. He

saw nothing but white. He tried to yell, but no sound came out. All he could do was reach for Philip. Philip would help.

But when Jack stretched out his hand, he grasped nothing.

He coughed and spat. Around him, the dust settled. The room gathered form. The foremast had broken off at the engine room bulkhead, and the crosstree joint rested firmly on the back of Jack's leg. He twisted around, trying to sit up, but the angle was bad. He couldn't possibly get enough leverage to lift the thing off.

Philip was gone. So was the sack of biscuits.

"Phili-i-i-i-p!"

Footsteps rumbled across the remains of the deck above him. "Father?" Colin called down.

"Down here! Under the mast!"

Colin leaped down. So did Mansfield, Flummerfelt, and Rivera. In moments they were squatting beside the mast, lifting it upward. And so was Philip.

Philip hadn't run away. He'd run to get help.

The release of the mast seemed to ignite Jack's leg. He grimaced, clamping his jaw against the pain.

Colin and Flummerfelt knelt beside him and

35

hoisted him up by the shoulders. "Tell me where it hurts," Colin said.

It hurt *everywhere*. "I'm . . . okay. Thank you. And you . . . Philip."

Philip nodded uncertainly.

Colin climbed abovedecks on the slanted foremast, then reached down as Rivera and Mansfield hoisted Jack over their heads. Once on deck, Jack leaned on his son, hobbling down the gangplank to a rousing *hip hip hooray* from the gathered crew.

He would have enjoyed it if he hadn't at that moment seen the starboard side of the *Mystery*.

It wasn't the hole — that remained more or less the same size. The hull itself had changed. It was warped. The pressure, unable to puncture a deeper hole, was instead squeezing the *Mystery* like a snake around a rat.

A wood plank came flying over the gunwale, and then another. Rivera was still on board, salvaging wood from the wreckage.

Not a good idea.

Captain Barth was at Jack's side, his face red. "What is he doing?"

"*Enough, Rivera!*" Jack shouted.

Rivera gazed down. "This is oak! We can use it!"

"*Get down here right this —*"

The earth slipped.

The guts of the *Mystery* — afterhold, engine room, fo'c'sle, and deckhouse — erupted through the deck in a black cloud of wood and twisted metal.

And the ship began to sink.

5

Colin

January 10, 1910

A piece of the tiller landed to his left. A mangled pipe from the engine room. A push broom.

The *Mystery* was dying.

Colin heard the voices shout and the dogs howl. He felt his body move. But he wasn't there. He was sinking, too.

"Get away!"

"Move back to the camp!"

"Last of ebb, and daylight waning . . ."

"Oppenheim, stop yammering and help out!"

"Mansfield's been hit!"

"Where's Rivera?"

"Has anyone seen Rivera?"

Mansfield had been clipped on the head by a flying piece of kennel. But he was breathing. Colin could see that because he had his hands under Mansfield's arms, dragging him away from the ship.

The half ship. That was all he could see now. Half. The hole that he and Kennedy had planned to fix was below the ice, wedged into the bent hull of the *Mystery*, now gutted and grotesque.

"Colin, this way — the infirmary tent."

"Siegal found Rivera! He's okay!"

"*Away to the boundless waste, and never again return!*"

"Someone tie Oppenheim down!"

Colin stooped to pick up a scrap of wood — a finger-sized splinter from one of the masts. It was attached to a grommet, a metal loop with a length of rope still knotted to it.

He closed his fingers over it and began to weep.

All the voices around him seemed to stop at once, and he felt his father's arm settle perfectly on his shoulder. But Colin wouldn't open his eyes, he didn't want to watch her go. The painted name, the gunwales, the taffrail, and finally the smokestack — that would be the order.

She had brought them into this world. She had kept them warm, sheltered them. When fourteen of her sons ventured out she'd waited for them, stalwart and steadfast.

They'd taken her example, her toughness, dignity, and grace. In return, they loved and cared for her. Over time, the soul of the *Mystery* — companion, protector, friend, mother — had become theirs.

Now she was leaving. Stranding them.

It was a feeling all too unfathomable and familiar.

Tears had frozen his eyes shut. He removed a glove and carefully cracked the ice off his lashes. The other men stood around the camp in small groups, facing the *Mystery*. Some had removed their hats and bowed their heads, and some openly sobbed.

"You can stand, Father?" Colin said softly.

"As long as I'm leaning on you." Father's eyes seemed gray and prematurely old. They frightened Colin.

Kosta's scream broke the silence. *"Ta skylakia! Ta skylakia!"*

The dogs.

They were out of control, scared, fighting and yowling. A group of them, at least half a dozen, had run away, becoming small dots on the horizon.

"Where're those mutts going?" said Talmadge.

"Don't matter," Windham replied. "Dogs always come back."

Bailey shook his head. "Comin' back is *normal* dog instinct. This ain't normal. They think they're going to die. Something's tellin' 'em to run. Look at the Greek, he knows it. Kiss 'em good-bye, mates."

"*Pericles! Michalaki! Eleni! Ellàtteh!*" Kosta shouted after the runaways. "*Paithia-a-a-a!*"

"*Combustion, blast, cloud, and vapor!*" wailed Oppenheim, shaking his fist at the sky.

Nigel, his face red, hurled debris wildly toward the horizon. "Stay away, you mongrel traitors! You ain't done nothin' but foul the decks 'n' eat our meat!"

Kosta limped toward the horizon, his shouts growing into screams. Andrew took his arm and tried to guide him back to the tent. O'Malley and Sanders threw chunks of ice at the *Mystery*, yelling incoherently. Blaming her. Blowing off steam.

A number of crewmen, shell-shocked, looked silently toward Captain Barth and Jack.

"What now?" asked Ruppenthal.

"We take a train," Brillman said.

"Is that supposed to be funny?" snapped Hayes.

"Have we no radio?" asked Philip. "No telephone?"

41

Windham glowered at him. "Let me just check my pockets."

"We traveled out of radio range near South America," Bailey explained. "Where were you, Philip?"

"In steerage with Nigel," Ruppenthal said, "eating our food and plotting our overthrow."

Captain Barth cut them off. "I need men immediately to go after those dogs. Those of you intent on preserving chaos and strife may go with them and keep on walking. We need the dogs more than you."

"Men, this —" Father's voice caught, and he cleared his throat. "This is a horror. No less. We must talk plainly — and act together, decisively, with eyes clear and hearts open. Let O'Malley and Sanders and Nigel alone for now. I'll handle them. Siegal, Stimson, Talmadge, and Windham, go after the dogs. The rest of you gather wood and debris — we'll make use of it all. Nesbit, help Drs. Montfort and Riesman in the infirmary. And as always, do whatever Captain Barth says."

The four dog chasers took off. The others trudged away to their tasks.

Colin was shaking. "Can we do this, Father?"

"Can we breathe and think?"

"The men are falling apart. They've lost their spirit already."

Barth nodded. "Without the ship, they're not sailors. The chain of command doesn't hold."

"They're men," Father replied. "They *want* a chain of command. And a plan of action. I suggest we stay put, shore up the camp. The winds and currents will carry the floes clockwise. We'll float our way around the sea, west by northwest. It worked for Fridtjof Nansen in the Arctic. In the meantime, we use the wood to build up our lifeboats and rig them. When we reach water, we sail out of here."

"Will we survive a winter down here?" Captain Barth replied. "Have you spotted many seals? Penguins? There aren't a whole lot here. Fewer in the winter — *they'll* be heading north. And when that sun goes away for three months, we won't even see the ones that remain."

"Why don't we do as the seals do?" Colin spoke up. "Head north over the ice. We can pull the camp after us."

"Pull the sledges *and* four lifeboats?" Barth asked. "Better to split into two teams — one to travel north, unladen, to check for leads, the other to stay put."

Father shook his head. "We're doomed if we

split, Elias. Under no circumstances will I allow that, ever. Whatever happens, we remain together."

"Aye, aye," Captain Barth said gravely.

"I agree with Colin," Father continued. "We must move — for the sake of morale as well as the hope of rescue."

"And when we reach the water?" Barth asked.

Father exhaled hard. "We'll worry about that when we come to it."

The runaway dogs — Chionni, Dimitriou, Eleni, Megalamatia, Michalaki, Pericles, Plutarchos, Sounion, and Zeus — were never found. The four men came back empty-handed.

Kosta took the news hard. But like the others, he worked through to the next day without stop. The only indication of night was a brief winking of the sun at the horizon line before it began its ascent. No one showed any desire to sleep, and no one complained of the toil.

No one wanted to talk at all.

Colin worked with Kennedy on the rebuilding of the lifeboat the *Horace Putney*. Under Kennedy's guidance, other teams worked on the *Raina*, the *Samuel Breen*, and the *Iphigenia*.

Using planks from the *Mystery*, Kennedy

taught Colin how to build up the sides, layering and nailing down planks lengthwise above the gunwale, following the curvature of the hull. This would protect the men better and prevent the boats from shipping water. The height would create an angle that would make rowing difficult, but Kennedy figured they'd have plenty of wind with which to sail.

Flummerfelt, Petard, and Siegal had been put to work fashioning four masts out of the wood Rivera had salvaged. To help move the boats over the ice, Windham and Bailey were making runners on removable frames, one set for each boat, based on Kennedy's carefully written blueprints.

The *Mystery* did not sink that week, not entirely. Squeezed by the sideways pressure, the remains of the mizzen and mainmast stuck upward, spindly and misshapen like dead trees.

To Colin, it seemed to linger like an unhappy spirit.

By then, Lombardo was on his feet a couple of hours per day. Kosta was learning how to ski with special bindings made by Kennedy, to accommodate his lack of toes.

Oppenheim, however, was deteriorating. He'd taken to wandering away from the camp with little clothing on, reciting poetry. At first Andrew had tried to handle him — thinking perhaps he had special soulful insight, no doubt. Soon Captain Barth assigned tougher men, Robert and Nigel, to the task.

Back home, Oppenheim had been a naval officer turned English teacher. Wanting to return to the sea and write a novel, he'd quit the job. If his classroom demeanor had been anything like it was now, Colin was relieved for the youth of America.

"Bring me my bow of burning gold," Oppenheim railed at the sky. *"Bring me my arrows of desire!"*

"Bring me some peace and quiet, blast it!" Nigel said. "Can't you ever shut your mouf, ya bloomin' lunatic?"

Oppenheim whirled around at him. "*Mouf* wif an F! You get an F! You fail! We all fail! And wasn't it predestined? Wasn't it? What is the future but the past seen through a mirror darkly?"

Nigel began applauding sarcastically. "Shakespeare, ain't it?"

"No, Oppenheim!"

"Lovely. Deserves a bleedin' prize. Per'aps you can save yer performances for the penguins, if we ever see any."

Robert let out a muffled oath. The commotion was making him lose concentration as he tried to attach a boom to the base of the *Raina*'s mast. "Gentlemen, please!" he called out.

"And wha' d'yer fink *you're* doin'?" Nigel asked. "Yer don't use *that size* bolts for the job. Too rigid, like. You need *flexitude*! Here, 'old the mast up."

Nigel grabbed Robert's can of bolts and threw them into the snow. Quickly, with great assurance, he began taking apart the joint and refitting it.

"Are you *sure* you know what you're doing?" Robert asked.

"I may be a stowaway to you, but I'm a professional sailor! Trust me, I've done this a fousand times."

No one — not a man alive — was as patient as Robert.

Turning back to his job, Colin brought his paintbrush to the stove. On the burner was a lukewarm pot of blackish liquid. Boiled seal's blood worked well in the absence of caulk or glue. Colin had quickly become expert at slathering the stuff with speed and skill.

On the morning of the seventh day, they built wooden decking over the bow sections of each lifeboat, then covered the decking with canvas. The construction was done.

The men loaded up the sledges and harnessed

the dogs. To the lifeboats they fastened harnesses and traces for themselves, made from rigging.

Into the *Horace Putney* were put two cots. Lombardo lay on one. Oppenheim was strapped to the other.

Jack gathered the men. "We'll split into three teams," he announced. "Mine will go first, to scout for a clear path. We will stay within sight. On cloudy days we will lay cairns of ice and rocks — whatever we find — and if visibility worsens we'll stay still until the others join us, at which time we'll tether all three teams with guy lines before we proceed. Captain Barth's team will follow mine; it will be the largest and will pull the two smaller lifeboats. The last team, led by Mansfield and Colin, will take the infirmary sledge."

As he read the names of each team, the men arranged themselves by their boats and sledges. As Colin fastened a harness around himself, Andrew took the one next to him.

"Godspeed," Andrew said.

"Just pull your weight," Colin replied.

"Readyyyy . . ." Captain Barth shouted. "Go-o-o-o!"

"*Yyyyya-a-a-ah!*" Colin bellowed, leaning forward into the traces.

The boat didn't budge.

"Harder!" Colin yelled. "Come on, Andrew! *Yyyyy-a-a-a-h!*"

There. It was beginning to edge ahead. Slowly. Very slowly.

"My rights are being violated!" Oppenheim shouted from behind them. "I demand to see the provost at once or I quit!"

"Shut up or I'll smack your provost from here to Canarsie!" Lombardo said.

The snow began to fall, slowly at first, then picking up speed.

When Colin looked over his shoulder, the *Mystery* was gone.

Part Two
Alone

6

Andrew

January 17, 1910

"I'm down!" Andrew cried out.

He picked himself up, brushing the snow from his trousers as he reset his skis into their tracks. His thighs were still wet and aching from the last fall.

"Again?" Colin called.

The *Horace Putney* jerked ahead, its runners crunching through the packed snow. Colin, Nigel, Robert, Hayes, Mansfield, Dr. Riesman, and Dr. Montfort pulled like a team of packhorses. Andrew was alone, "resting." All the men had three rest periods throughout the day, according to a schedule Colin had worked out. You either pulled or you skied.

They'd worked out a system of calls and responses. It was *Down* if you'd fallen but remained in control. *Avast-ho!* if you'd fallen and needed help. *Hey-o-o-o!* to start the team back up when you were back on your feet. Three long whistles for an emergency. One long whistle, two short, if you spotted a seal or a penguin. And so on.

If you called out, someone on the team was supposed to acknowledge by echoing you.

Not by saying, *Again?*

Andrew tightened his bindings and began moving forward. The bottoms of his skis had been waxed stingily at the beginning of the day. Now that the snowfall had turned wet, they were sticking.

Some rest period.

"Hey-o-o-o!" he yelled.

"Hey-o-o-o!" one of the men yelled back.

The wind stung his face and blew snow down his neck despite a tightly wrapped scarf. Aside from the wetness, the weather had changed little during the four days, the terrain not at all. The hummocks and ridges were beginning to look familiar to Andrew. He had the frightening sensation the teams were going around in circles.

As Andrew caught up to the *Horace Putney*, he caught a glimpse of Oppenheim, riding inside the boat. He wore no goggles but his back was to the wind, and he stared with steely eyes into the distance, his arms rigidly to his side and his palms facing up, as if serving an invisible meal.

He'd been this way for two days.

"Me back is breakin', mate!" Nigel complained. "I need a rest."

"Keep pulling," Colin shot back.

"Gar, wha' d'yer fink I am, a beask of burden? Your brother 'ad 'is nice ski trip — why can't we switch places?"

"We're supposed to *make up* ground during Andrew's breaks," Colin replied.

"Nigel, you should be glad we didn't leave you behind," Hayes snarled.

"You're lucky I haven't snapped you in half!" cried Lombardo from within the *Horace Putney*. "Or sicced Oppenheim on you."

"No comments from the luxury seats," growled Nigel. "An' keep an eye out for the yeti."

"The *who*?" Lombardo asked.

"Big, 'airy creature. Lives in the ice caves 'n' eats people. True story. I 'eard about it in India or Nepal or some bloody place."

Lombardo began warbling in a huge voice:

"O-o-o-oh, I-I-I'm a Yeti Doodle Dandy, a Ye-e-eti Doodle Do or Di-i-ie!"

"Stop it — 'e'll 'ear you!"

Andrew wanted to swat Colin for his comment. *Make up ground* during Andrew's breaks? That was snide.

He counted silently to the rhythm of his sliding skis.

Thirteen . . . fourteen . . .

It was insulting.

Fifteen . . . sixteen . . .

One minute Colin was decent and concerned, the next a snake. Why? How could someone who had saved his life turn like this?

The worst part of it was, Andrew couldn't say a thing. Bickering had no place. Survival was all — feeding the dogs, hunting, cooking, making temporary camp, navigating, pulling, resting.

The boat team was slowing down. The dogs, too. Wet snow stuck to the runners, and the ice was hummocky. Ahead of them, Captain Barth's team had stopped, both sledge and lifeboat tilted into a soupy mess.

"I can't do this anymore!" Nigel cried.

"I gotta agree with him," Hayes said. "This is horrible."

"No," Mansfield said. "It's beautiful."

"Oh, blimey, do we put you wif Oppenheim, now?" Nigel asked.

"Don't you see?" Mansfield said. "These conditions mean we're getting closer to open water. We'll pull up with Team Two and break for lunch. And watch for that crack ahead!"

The *Horace Putney* jolted over a sudden sharp ridge. Supplies crashed loudly inside the boat, and Lombardo let out a howl of pain.

The ice seemed to give a little.

In front of the ridge was a long crack in the ice, at least a foot wide, running directly across Andrew's path. It didn't seem too dangerous; the skis would easily traverse it. Nonetheless he slowed to a stop. You never knew.

He stepped forward with his right foot over the crack.

Solid. Not a problem.

His team was gaining on Team Two now, the men shouting at one another. Ruppenthal, on Captain Barth's team, had already set up a stove.

Andrew pushed forward, digging in his ski poles. His left leg slid over the crack.

A black shadow shot across his vision, under the ice.

Andrew tried to react but couldn't possibly.

The head burst through the crack in a geyser of gray. Jaws opened quickly, baring jagged teeth for only a moment.

Andrew had no time to scream before the teeth closed over his calf and dragged him under.

7

Colin

Colin flew.

Lunging, he gripped Andrew by the arm and pulled. Out of the crack emerged a monstrous head, domelike and water-glistened, flecked with spots of black. Its mouth clung firmly to Andrew's leg.

For a moment its eyes appraised Colin with cold indifference. Then, with a violent lurch, it pulled down.

Andrew fell toward the crack, yanking Colin off balance. *"Get it off get it off get it yyahhhhhh!"*

It was a killer. A predator. Trained to hunt by spying prey from under the ice, then ambushing.

Well, not this prey.

Colin planted his feet in the snow and held his brother tight.

Flummerfelt loomed above them. He raised a two-by-four and swiftly struck down. The plank splashed into the crack, sending up a gusher of water that froze as it struck Colin's face.

Colin heard a dull, wet thud.

"*HYEEEEEAH!*" Flummerfelt struck repeatedly with ferocious strength. "*HYEEEEAH! HYEEEEAH!*"

"*My leg! My leg!*" Andrew screamed.

The water coated Colin's goggles, now darkening to pink, then red.

The other men closed around fast. Shouting through gritted teeth, they struck with more wood like a team of crazed pile drivers, their red eyes bulging, their red necks veiny and thick.

Under the barrage, the creature weakened. Mansfield grabbed Andrew and helped Colin pull.

Andrew's leg slowly emerged. The monster's head reappeared, a battered mass, blackened by blood, its spots now undetectable. Still attached to Andrew.

The thing wasn't giving up. Its head must have been made of steel.

"*KILL IT! KILL I-I-I-IT!*" the men shouted, bludgeoning the creature with renewed force.

Finally its eyes turned toward them. It stared for a long moment, unflinching against the onslaught, as if memorizing their features for future reference.

Then, without ceremony, it let go its jaws and sank into the water.

Andrew fell back, knocking over Mansfield and Colin.

The men continued striking, their frenzy unabated. Below them a shadow glided under the ice and disappeared.

"*It hurts!*" Andrew cried, writhing and kicking.

"Lie still, Andrew!" Dr. Montfort commanded, ripping open Andrew's trouser leg. "Someone get more water. I can't see the wound."

Colin tore off his leather cap, scooped bloody water from the crack, and poured it over Andrew's leg.

Andrew howled with pain. "*What are you doing to me?*"

The gash was long and ugly. Dr. Montfort ripped a length of material from his own shirt and made a tourniquet, tying it above the wound. "Give me some pressure here, Colin."

Colin leaned on his brother's leg.

"*Stop it, Colin!*"

"Ssssh, Andrew, it's okay."

"Leather winter breeches," Dr. Montfort muttered, "three pairs of moleskin pants . . . long underwear . . . he wore all his clothes. That fact may save his leg. I think the bite was more crush than tear."

The other men still stood around the crack, shattering chunks of ice and bellowing like madmen. They were all soaked with water now, their drab clothing darkened to a black-red.

"*Avast, men!*" Captain Barth shouted. "Winslow is returning! Avast before he sees you!"

The men slowly subsided. Their faces were drained and bewildered. They looked toward Andrew as if just remembering he still existed.

As Colin helped Dr. Montfort lay Andrew on a cot, a team went to work building a tent around them. Andrew was unconscious now, snoring, and Colin propped his head up on a pillow made from shirts and underwear.

This was Colin's fault. Andrew shouldn't have been skiing. His rest period had ended at least fifteen minutes earlier. Technically, it had been *Colin's* turn. But he had let Andrew continue. If he had done what he was supposed to do, he would have gone over that crack himself, not Andrew.

Colin had broken the rules because the team needed speed. But a leader didn't make arbitrary rules and then change them. A leader was steady. A leader led.

Perhaps Colin would have seen the beast. He'd have found a narrower break in the ice or alerted the others to distract it.

But it was too late.

"Bandage," Dr. Montfort said. "Now."

Colin ran outside and took a strip of snow-washed cloth that lay drying on the stove. Andrew was losing blood like crazy. If it weren't for the cold, he'd probably be dead.

Father's team was approaching now. The camp dogs yapped loudly, greeting the arrival. Colin's heart raced as he ducked back into the tent.

Dr. Montfort quickly removed Andrew's bandage. The blood was beginning to clot around the edges of the gash. The redness had spread through Andrew's thigh, and the entire leg was beginning to swell.

Father rushed in, out of breath. "What on earth happened?"

"This — *thing*," Colin blurted out. "A seal. It jumped out of the water and bit him. It tried to take him down, but I — Mansfield and I — pulled him out —"

Father flinched at the sight of the leg. "Will he lose it?"

Dr. Montfort shook his head. "I don't think so. It's pretty inflamed right now, and he's lost a bit of blood, but there's not much risk of infection down here in a land with no germs."

"Thank God." Father placed a hand on Andrew's forehead, feeling for a temperature.

"Without Colin, he might not have made it," Dr. Montfort said.

"That's not true," Colin replied.

"Oh, yes it is," said Bailey, his voice hoarse from shouting, his coat covered with blood.

From all sides, crew members crowded into the tent. "'E yanked 'im out wif 'is bare 'ands," Nigel said.

Hayes nodded. "That thing nearly pulled Andrew under."

"It was huge," Cranston said. "Maybe ten, twelve feet. Some prehistoric dinosaur-fish, like."

"Only Colin could have matched the strength of that thing," Mansfield said. "Well, maybe Flummerfelt."

"Don't look at me," Flummerfelt said. "I was scared."

Father smiled at Colin. "Andrew's a lucky boy to have a brother like you."

"I was the one who let him ski," Colin said, shaking his head.

The men stared as if they hadn't heard him, their eyes resolute, their faces blood-spattered.

Despair and hunger had changed them. They needed a hero. It was all black-and-white now. Evil and Good. Kill or be killed.

We are all animals inside, Colin's teacher used to say. Put to the test, we react like tigers. Civilization falls away, and all we're left with is instinct.

Civilization was the *Mystery*.

Dr. Riesman rushed into the tent, holding a leather-bound book. He knelt by Jack's side and opened it to a photo of a spotted seal. "A leopard seal. Carnivorous. Stalks its prey — penguins, usually — under the ice. When it sees a shadow, it follows patiently, sometimes swimming for miles. Then it waits by a nearby hole in the ice — perhaps a hole made by itself. When the prey steps over the open water, the seal attacks with incredible swiftness, usually crushing the head."

"So it thought Andrew was a penguin?" Windham asked.

"It didn't know what it had found," Dr. Riesman said. "Perhaps that's why its bite was not as . . . precise as it could have been."

Ruskey slipped between the men, focusing his camera on Andrew's leg. "Dr. Montfort, can you remove the bandage for a moment?"

"After it heals," Dr. Montfort replied.

"Dare I look?" Philip's voice piped up from a corner of the tent. "I don't know if I have the stomach for the sight of entrails."

"Will someone get him and Ruskey out of here?" Captain Barth snapped.

Colin stood up. The photographer nodded amiably and stepped outside. Philip followed, clutching an oddly shaped sack of hardtack.

Colin stood by the tent flap and scanned the ice. The clouds had begun to lift, and he saw the sun's orb for the first time in days. In the harsh light, the ice directly under them seemed darker than usual.

Water. Of course. The ice had to be pretty thin. How else could the leopard seal see through?

In the tent, the men were jabbering loudly about the incident. Father silently stepped away from them and walked over to Colin. "Do you see what I see?"

"Yeah, thin ice," Colin replied.

"I had to swerve the team to the east to avoid this floe. The pack must be breaking up."

"Will we be able to put in?"

"We didn't see leads — but that deep blue on the horizon is a water sky, and leopard seals don't stray far from the coast."

"That's great. Unless we fall through right here."

"This ice is still maybe three, four feet thick. It'll do unless the weather warms. We can move after Andrew's condition improves. I wouldn't travel much farther north-northwest, though."

Colin squinted toward the horizon. From behind a decaying pressure ridge, two figures wandered out over the ice. Philip and Ruskey.

From Colin's angle, the ice under them looked practically blue.

"What are they doing?" Father asked.

Colin raised his fingers to his lips and blasted three long whistles. They echoed loudly over the ice, borne on a stiff wind that had just started up from the south.

Ruskey continued on, snapping photos. Philip

stopped to wave, then scampered after Ruskey, dragging his sack behind him.

"The idiots!" Colin said.

"Let's get them," Father said.

They began to run. Colin let out another whistle, sharper and louder.

Philip stopped again.

He hadn't turned halfway around when he disappeared into the ice.

8

Philip

January 17, 1910

It happened fast. As if Philip's body had dropped clean away from its soul. Although he felt it all, he could see it, too — feet, legs, waist, chest, head submerging in slow motion. As his lungs seized up he heard the water smack over his head, like the sound of a doctor gently slapping a newborn. In the end as it was in the beginning.

And when the force began to lift him, Philip realized with horror that this was it. No more excuses. All sins were revealed on the Day of Reckoning, and what could he say for himself — that he hadn't meant to rob the bank, that it had been a silly game, that he'd suffered enough already in this frozen wasteland — and he felt the force lifting him heavenward, no doubt merely a backswing before pitching him downward to the place he'd always expected to go —

"*Pkkkkuaaachhhh!*"

Throwing up before the Pearly Gates. That would not do. Bad form.

"Philip, if you had twice as much intelligence you'd be a half-wit!"

"*Rrrrraaaauuuugh!*" He was spewing out water, his body convulsing on hard ice, his lungs frozen.

"Ruskey, put your coat over him!"

Colin's voice. Jack's.

Philip struggled to open his eyes. He was alive. The ice fell from his lashes, tinkling onto his cheek. He tried to speak, but his jaw was frozen. "I'ng . . . ngot . . . dead."

"One more second . . ." Colin said, out of breath, "and you'd have been food for a leopard seal."

"They'll have to settle for hardtack," Ruskey said.

"Ny vag!" Philip sat up. He retched out more saltwater. His lungs felt as if they'd been scraped with a wire brush.

Where was the bag? *Where were those bloody plates?*

"Where is ny v — al mmmmy bag?"

Nowhere. The hole — the blasted hole he'd fallen through — it was gone. The crack was sealed. Philip fell forward, clawing at the ice. He dug his fingers into the crack and tried to pull.

"Philip, are you crazy?" Colin said.

"You don't understand. I must have it!"

Colin yanked him away. "Philip, we are between two ice floes. Two *thin* ice floes. Any moment they could open up again!"

Ruskey handed his camera to Jack. "I'll take the feet. Colin, you get the shoulders."

The two younger men swooped down upon Philip, lifting him off the ice. He began to weep, but the tears became trapped behind globs of ice on his lashes, giving him a throbbing headache on top of all the other indignities.

This was a punishment, wasn't it? A salvo from the Almighty, a punishment for his bad deed.

It was unfair. He'd already *lost* the money. That was punishment enough. The photos had been *there*, unclaimed. Surely this one last act could have been overlooked?

The other crewmen were cheering outside the tents — all but the two medical doctors, who were tending to Andrew.

None of them saw the dismal truth. "My plates . . ." Philip moaned as Colin and Ruskey set him on a cot.

Immediately Dr. Montfort began wrapping him in tarps and blankets.

"Wha' did 'e say?" Nigel asked.

"Plates?" Nesbit said. "Dinner plates?"

"Just a moment," Ruskey said. "Westfall, what exactly was in that sack?"

The faces stared down at him, hard *sailors'* faces, full of fight and filth.

"Hardtack," he mumbled.

"Hardtack . . . with a little silver nitrate, maybe?" Ruskey said. "Big, *b-i-i-i-ig* flat biscuits with funny white-on-black images?"

"Ruskey, please —"

"You took my photographic plates — the ones I left on the *Mystery* because of the weight limit. Instead of evacuating as you were supposed to, you waited until I left and stuffed them into your sack."

"You common little feef!" Nigel blurted out. "You was '*idin*' the photogs so's you could sell 'em! Is there no end to your greed?"

"My greed?" Philip protested. "You're angry because *you* didn't think of it!"

Captain Barth was livid. "You disobeyed orders to evacuate, Westfall."

"When the foremast fell, Pop had to run back in for you," Mansfield said.

"He nearly died," Nesbit added.

They were advancing. Slowly. Like wolves around a poor little lamb.

Philip cowered. "Yes, well, I wasn't too happy with that turn of events myself."

"You are despicable," Pete Hayes growled, "sneaky, lazy, selfish, filthy —"

"I am *not* filthy!" Philip protested. "But I *am* sick and injured, and frightfully hungry —"

A twisted smile grew across Kennedy's face. "Say, I'm hungry, too, men . . . how about y'all?"

"Sure would be nice to have something besides seal, wouldn't it?" Ruppenthal said. "Somethin' tender and fat — you know, the way Philip is, on account of his hiding out in the storeroom, eating our good food."

"He sure looks like a well-fed pig," O'Malley added. "Prob'ly just as tasty, too."

Their jokes were sick. Simply disgusting.

Philip sat up. "Yes, I admit to a youthful zeal for

73

the photographic arts, and I deeply apologize if I have offended anyone — but it is hardly the occasion for such morbid humor."

"I imagine he'd be pretty soft," Sanders guessed.

"Oily, too," Cranston said.

Ruppenthal nodded. "You'd need a lot of barbecue sauce to cover the stink."

Barbarians. Visigoths. Cannibals.

Philip stood up, his blankets and tarps still draped around him, and backpedaled out of the tent. "M-m-m-may I remind you, s-s-sirs, we are *gentlemen*. We can s-s-s-settle our hunger issues like rational, courteous b-b-beings —"

"*LU-U-U-UNCH!*" cried Ruppenthal.

Like slavering beasts, they sprang.

Philip spun. He bolted away.

He hadn't seen the stove directly behind him.

He slammed against it and fell to the ice in a clatter of coal, wood, and blubber-blackened steel. "Stop! This is inhuman! I am not edible! *I am an Englishman!*"

He rolled himself into a ball and braced for the sacrifice.

But the men did not come nearer.

Philip parted his elbows. Cautiously he peeked out.

Flummerfelt was the first to laugh — a long, brutish *Hawwww* most likely honed to perfection on some hog farm in Iowa.

The men erupted, doubling over, slapping one another's backs and pointing. Rejoicing at his humiliation — as if he were some cheap vaudeville performer. Even Lombardo and the Greek were up and about, enjoying a guffaw or two at his expense.

"Gotcha, didn't we?" Sanders brayed.

Philip stood up. He calmly brushed himself off. He would not let them see his embarrassment. Even though his clothes were frozen through and his entire body felt bruised and stiff, he still had his dignity.

"I didn't believe you," he said. "Not for a moment."

He was dreaming of plum pudding with heavy cream when the dogs woke him next morning. One of the larger ones — Agamemnon or Hypocrite or some blasted Greek name — was licking his face, slobbering bacteria into every cut and pimple.

Philip sat up. He felt as if his head had been smacked between cement blocks.

He lay back down.

They were all bustling around him. They were always bustling.

"Fifteen minutes for breakfast, and then into the traces, men!" Captain Barth shouted.

"Thank you," Philip grumbled, "but I think I'll stay here."

Colin sat next to him. "How are you feeling?"

"So kind of you to ask. Dreadful."

"Ready to pull, or do we need to put you in the boat with Lombardo, Andrew, and Oppenheim?"

"Anything but Oppenheim."

Colin smiled. "You're a lot tougher than I gave you credit for. Andrew's dead to the world."

"Andrew was bitten. I merely froze." Philip slowly rose to his feet, his shirtsleeve falling far down over his hands. "You gave me your clothes yesterday, didn't you?"

"They were spares."

"After that cruel treatment I received, you fed me and made sure I was warm. I shan't forget that."

"Look, it wasn't a proposal of marriage, Philip. I was looking out for Andrew, and you happened to be in the tent, too."

"Thanks anyway."

Colin gave him a half smile, then ran off to breakfast.

Humanity lived, after all, in Camp Perseverance.

The penguin pemmican tasted especially foul this morning, the coffee like charcoal. The teams were already hitching their dogs to the sledges, and men had begun slipping into their traces.

Andrew lay on a cot, alone on the *Horace Putney*. Lombardo had insisted on skiing.

"Philip, when you finish dining, take the harness next to Oppenheim," Mansfield said. "He's giving it a try today."

Philip's heart sank.

Oppenheim turned toward him with a wide smile. *"I'm going to ride the chariot in the morning, Lord! Oh, I'm getting ready for the Judgment Day. . . ."*

Three hours of hard labor with a madman.

Philip took a bite of penguin pemmican and chewed. Slowly.

The clouds had rolled in again overnight, hiding the sun and the horizon. He wished he could roll away with them.

Everything of value to him was gone — the money, the photographs, his pride. What was the point of going home? Mum had gotten rid of him. Uncle Horace couldn't stand the sight of him. The only people who wanted him were the police; they'd be waiting with open shackles.

Of course, he could escape after landing, as

Nigel had proposed — but then what? Hop Argentine freighters . . . with *Nigel*? Pick bananas in Honduras?

Colin should have let him sink. No one would have shed a tear. For the first time in his life, he'd have brought a little good into the world.

"'Ay, Philip, whatcher waitin' for, an engraved imitation?" Nigel yelled. "We need yer sorry carcass!"

Philip spat out the pemmican, walked to the boat, and picked up his traces.

9

Jack

"*Avast — ho!*" Jack cried out.

He was exhausted and short of breath. The sweat stung bitterly when it dripped into his eyes, and it left a brackish taste on his lips.

The air had changed. It was sea air, and he'd smelled it miles away. Anyone who knew the sea could detect its fragrance in the unlikeliest of places — in the grimy industrial air of New York City and the bone-dry California deserts, in the rainy mountains of Washington State and the dusty Texas plains.

Salt had no odor, and neither did water — but

together with the rotting algae, the fish carcasses, and the mold in the air, the scent was unmistakable.

To a sailor, it was perfume.

All three teams slowed to a halt. The ice here was crisscrossed with webbed footprints, the distant ridges lined with penguins, gulls, and terns. A lone skua swooped overhead, screaming. In the distance, a gliding bird plummeted from the sky toward its prey below.

The dogs yapped madly, lurching toward the birds, pulling the sledges in all directions.

Over the last two days, the pulling had become almost impossible. The wet snow clung to the soles of Jack's boots, and his team had nearly lost the *Raina* when its runners caught in a field of hummocks.

Not far ahead of them were three good leads, long fingers of deep blue water thrusting through the surface. Maybe a half mile farther, the floes broke up into choppy brash ice. Beyond that would be open sea.

"This is as far as we go," Jack announced.

"I could have told you that," Siegal said.

Mansfield thrust a fist into the air. "Hip hip —"

"Feet feet," Ruppenthal grumbled, "shoulders shoulders, knees knees — they all hurt."

The men unhooked themselves and sat on the

ice, one by one, as O'Malley and Stimson untied the food bags. A few of the men — Colin, Mansfield, Barth, Siegal, Kennedy — seemed relieved, but most were too tired to react.

Of the sick men, Kosta and Lombardo were doing the best. Oppenheim, however, was hurling oaths and chunks of ice back in the direction they'd come.

Jack walked back to the *Horace Putney* with Captain Barth. "How's Andrew?"

"Sleeping," Colin said.

Dr. Montfort nodded reassuringly. "The gash is healing well. It wasn't as deep as I'd feared. No broken bones or torn ligaments — he'll have a whopping bruise for a while, but that's about it. He's one lucky kid."

"Brave, too," said Captain Barth.

Jack nodded. Andrew would need bravery. And good health.

What came next would require both in spades.

"What now, Father?" Colin asked.

"We can't stay here," Jack said. "The ice isn't stable enough — especially if the weather turns warmer."

"We have to decide something fast, Jack," Captain Barth said. "To keep the peace."

Raised voices echoed from the men's encampment — Lombardo and Ruppenthal, Nigel and Philip, Oppenheim and Rivera — arguing, taunting, everyone at the end of his tether.

Jack reached into his pocket and pulled out a small American flag wrapped around a crumpled, water-soaked sheet of paper. Carefully he unfolded the paper and read the India ink inscription on top.

For Jack Winslow, fellow traveler,
kindred spirit,
May your sails always be trimmed to a
freshening wind —
Godspeed,
Lawrence "Chappy" Walden,
cartographer

Below it was a neatly drawn map of Antarctica, the coasts in great topographical detail, the interior a blank expanse of white.

Walden had planned to map every inch of the Antarctic shoreline. He would move slowly, returning to the mainland for fuel when necessary.

The two men had met in Argentina. For good

luck, each had agreed to give the other a souvenir. Walden had given Jack the flag and the map. Jack, distracted by problems, had returned nothing — and had been haunted by that ever since. A broken gesture had power. It worked on your mind in quiet ways, weakening your resolve and your courage.

Now the map might come in handy.

"Gather, men!" Jack called out.

"What's the plan?" Ruppenthal called out.

"Put to and sail out of here, I'll bet," Siegal said.

"We can't sail these dinghies in this mess," Windham said. "We'll capsize."

"Pop, I say retreat to a stabler floe and wait out the summer," Mansfield suggested. "In a couple of months the Ross Sea will freeze up right to the ocean, which'll give us another fifty miles or so of ice —"

"A couple of months?" Cranston snapped. "We can't survive here that long!"

"Death never takes the wise man by surprise," Oppenheim shouted. *"He is always ready to go!"*

"Listen up — I have Chappy Walden's map and itinerary," Jack announced. "He left three weeks after we did, sailing west to circumnavigate Antarctica and map the coast. He drew his route for me on this sheet, pinpointing dates and locations. If he has stuck to his schedule, he should be approaching the Ross Sea right around now."

"So . . . we stay here and wait for him?" Philip asked.

"Right, and wave to 'im wif our 'ankies?" Nigel said. "Yoo-hoo! Captain Wa-a-a-alden!"

"Staying here, we have little chance of seeing him or being seen," Jack said. "If we sail now, making our way slowly through the brash —"

"And bergs," Mansfield interrupted.

"— we'll reach the shelf ice in two or three days. Fewer if we're lucky. One thing we know about Walden — he'll be hugging the coast. Chances are good we'll cross paths."

"*How* close to the shore?" Oppenheim blurted out. "Can anyone really know that?"

The commotion stopped, and all eyes turned to Oppenheim.

"What are the *real* odds of two vessels actually crossing paths in this vast sea?" Oppenheim pressed on. "And what if we *don't* find him? We marry the penguins and settle in?"

He was making sense. His words were brutal and honest.

Looking at Oppenheim's face, Jack realized

that "crazy" was an easy label. Oppenheim was a rational man with an impossible task — to function as a human without any hope and faith. In his eyes, Jack saw the despair of every man in the crew. And, possibly, their future.

"If all else fails," Jack said, "we make our way along the western coast until we reach the Antarctic peninsula — which we will follow north to Deception Island. There we'll find a whaling station."

"How many miles away is Deception Island?" Andrew chimed in from the *Horace Putney.*

The crew turned. Andrew was sitting up with great effort.

Jack wished he could greet him with good news. Instead he told the truth. "About twenty-five hundred."

"Impossible!" Bailey said.

"Gar!" Nigel shouted. "In *lifeboats?*"

"My good man, that is the entire length of your country," Philip said, "give or take a state or two."

"Father, how can we possibly do this?" Colin asked.

Oppenheim began to pace back and forth. *"We all labour against our own cure, for death is the cure of all diseases."*

"It has been done," Jack said confidently, "by

lesser men than we. It is our *backup* plan, remember. We'll start tomorrow morning."

The men studied his face. He kept a confident cut of the jaw, an upbeat expression.

Confidence was the key.

The journey *hadn't* been done. It was impossible.

But that didn't matter. Walden was out there.

And they would find him.

Part Three

Launch

1 0

Colin

February 5, 1910

"Heeeeave-ho-o-o!"

Colin gave a solid push and the *Horace Putney* slid off its runners. Its bow slapped into the water.

Day one.

If he thought about it, he would count the men and dogs — thirty and thirteen — and then count the boats — four — and he would imagine those four lifeboats on the same savage sea that had battered the *Mystery*. All heading off to die foolishly.

If he thought about it.

But so much had to be done — checking and packing and discarding and rigging and rounding up — that he could easily choose not to think about it at all.

"We can't fit the seal chops!" O'Malley shouted.

"Toss 'em or eat 'em now!" Captain Barth replied. "We're only packing penguin hoosh, hard-tack, and pemmican! We'll anchor and hunt when the need arises."

"Can't anyone get these bloody pigeons away?" Philip shouted, shooing a bird away from a chunk of meat cooking on the stove.

"They ain't *pigeons*, ya blighter — they's sea-gulls!" Nigel said.

RRRROWFF! Socrates lunged at a tern, knocking over the stove. The meat fell to the guano-covered rocks.

"My seal!" Philip whined.

"We could fit the meat in the boats if we didn't have the dogs," Ruppenthal snarled.

"Don't start in about them again," Talmadge said.

The dogs had been a problem. A couple of the men had wanted to abandon them. But Jack had said no, they come, too.

The stove and many of their supplies would be left behind. The men would take two Primus stoves,

Ruskey's photographic plates, weapons for hunting, buckets for bailing, string and frozen seal blood for repairs, a Bible, lots of extra wood — and, of course, ballast. With the weight so evenly spread port-to-starboard, the boats would need to be ballasted properly to prevent heeling.

No extra clothes.

"Dogs first, then men!" Jack cried out.

"*Socrates! Demosthenes! Iosif! Kalliope!*"

Socrates ran for the *Samuel Breen*. The others ran away.

"*Ellàteh, paithià mou!*"

Socrates leaped. His front legs locked onto the gunwale, but he fell back into the water, dousing Nesbit.

Demosthenes jumped on Socrates. Kalliope jumped on Nesbit.

"Get this thing off me!" Nesbit shouted.

Mansfield let out a whoop. "This is war!"

The men ran after the dogs, picking them up one by one and depositing them in the boats.

One by one, the dogs jumped out.

Lombardo fell to the ice as Fotis licked his face. Ireni began digging a hole. Nikola bayed at an albatross.

It took the better part of a half hour to get the dogs settled. By then everyone was soaked and in high spirits.

Except Philip. Philip was dry and miserable. "I request a canine-free vessel," he said.

"You're coming with me in the *Horace Putney*," Jack said, reading from a handwritten list, "along with Colin, Mansfield, Cranston, Sanders, and Kennedy."

Philip?

Colin couldn't believe it. As Father turned for the boat, Colin elbowed him. "Why'd you pick *Philip*?"

"For his protection," Jack replied. "If I put him on any other boat, the men'll kill him."

Now the opportunity's all mine, Colin thought.

Jack gathered the men into a circle. He linked arms with Colin on one side and Andrew on the other.

One by one, the others locked arms, too.

"We are a chain," Jack said. "We must stay together, *in each other's sight*, at all costs. We're loaded beyond any reasonable standards. Exercise *extreme* caution. If we separate — if one boat is damaged — our return voyage is doomed. With God's help, we'll find Walden soon. I believe that with all my soul."

Silence greeted the speech, but no words were needed. In glances and facial tics, posture and movement, the men spoke volumes. Despair for the unreasonable, hope for the impossible.

The boats now lay half in the water. Colin committed the personnel of each to memory. The dogs were already in: Ireni, Maria, and Stavros in the *Horace Putney*; Kalliope, Fotis, and Martha in the *Iphigenia*; Demosthenes, Socrates, and Yiorgos in the *Samuel Breen*; and Kristina, Iosif, Nikola, and Panagiotis in the *Raina*.

Into the *Iphigenia* climbed Rivera, Riesman, Talmadge, Windham, O'Malley, Flummerfelt, Ruppenthal, Ruskey.

The *Samuel Breen*: Siegal, Nesbit, Petard, Brillman, Stimson, Bailey, Hayes.

The *Raina*: Barth, Andrew, Montfort, Kosta, Lombardo, Oppenheim, Robert, and Nigel.

Some would be standing — there was no way to prevent that. The dogs would have to lie on the ballast and in men's laps. And Father had made it clear that the personnel should switch boats regularly at each stop along the coast.

Colin gave the *Horace Putney*'s stern a hard push until it was afloat, then jumped in himself.

The boat rocked on a strong, choppy current.

The brash ice billowed against the hull, making a noise like crunching gravel. Cranston took the tiller as Colin and Jack used oars to push against the larger blocks of ice, guiding the boat northeast, toward a break near the horizon.

"Oh, I believe I am getting sick," Philip moaned.

The dogs whined, moving around in circles. Colin was jammed against the starboard hull and had poor leverage.

The boat was uncomfortable. Badly balanced. Slow.

And thrilling.

The land had not been kind. The sea was a friend; the sea had gotten them here alive, and now perhaps it would deliver them.

The current pulled the boats steadily northwest, aided by a sharp crosswind. They were headed for a field of freshly calved icebergs, about three-quarters of a mile away.

"Set the sails!" Father called out.

Kennedy and Mansfield scrambled to unlash the sail and lower the boom. "Ready about!" Kennedy cried, pulling the sheet.

The *Iphigenia* was directly behind them. The

Raina and the *Samuel Breen* had drifted west and were tacking to catch up.

"It doesn't look like we're getting away from those bergs!" Cranston shouted.

"The bergs are moving, too," Jack replied.

"Shouldn't they be moving the other way?" Kennedy asked.

"Must be some kind of crosscurrent," Mansfield said. "Watch for a strong riptide — or whirlpool."

A cloud cover had developed in the south, over the Antarctic plain. It loomed behind the other three boats, growing fast.

"Jibe to the east and be prepared to lower sails!" Father shouted.

The wind was at their backs, forcing them to zigzag in order to catch a good crosswind. For a good forty-five minutes, Colin watched the cloud gradually turn black. It swallowed the *Raina* and *Samuel Breen* first, then quickly engulfed the *Iphigenia*.

"Bring her around and heave to! On the double!" Jack commanded. *"READY ABOUT!"*

Philip ducked under the forward decking. Mansfield and Kennedy released the sheet and let the boom swing again.

They trimmed the sail and brought the *Horace*

Putney about so that its bow faced into the wind. Again they let the sheet loose and the sail went slack. As the two men secured the sail, Sanders kept a firm grip on the rudder, making sure the boat stayed properly hove to.

The wind struck like a cannon. It blew rocks and ice into their faces and sent up swells that tossed the boat furiously.

Stavros began yowling from the bottom of the boat. Instantly the other dogs — and Philip — joined.

"Stay low!" Sanders called out.

Colin and Jack inserted their oars into the oar-locks. For stability they extended the oars, feathering them so that the blades rested flat on the water's surface.

"I see the *Iphigenia*!" Colin shouted.

He shielded his face, keeping his eyes on the place where he'd spotted the boat's silhouette. It peeked in and out of the fog, heaving to and tossing on the waves.

As the wind increased, the clouds began to blow off.

"Where are the other two?" Mansfield shouted.

The *Iphigenia* had held position fast. But the *Raina* and the *Samuel Breen* were nowhere in sight.

Colin scanned the horizon until he saw two specks emerging from behind the trailing edge of the fog. "Twenty-five degrees off the starboard bow!" he yelled. "Heading for that growler!"

Both ships lay across the wind. They were being blown straight into an iceberg.

11

Andrew

February 5, 1910

"*Set the sail!*" Captain Barth bellowed.

"The wind must be forty knots!" Andrew replied.

"I didn't ask for a weather report!" Barth held the tiller tightly, trying to point the boat in the direction of the *Samuel Breen*.

Fifty yards ahead of them, the *Breen* careened toward the berg. It was a small one, a growler, with maybe twenty feet showing above water. But Andrew knew that ninety percent of an iceberg's volume lay beneath the surface.

For a boat this size, in a wind this strong, it was deadly.

Andrew braced his leg against the deck. The

calf was wrapped in thick canvas and Dr. Montfort assured him it was healing well, but the pain was still excruciating.

He couldn't dwell on it. He was one of eight on this boat. And considering that Oppenheim was deadweight, Kosta wasn't much of a sailor, Lombardo was still weak, and Nigel was Nigel, Andrew knew he had to pull his weight.

He and Lombardo quickly unfurled the *Raina*'s sail. As it caught the wind, the boat swung hard to starboard.

With a loud smack, the *Raina* struck a pitted chunk of old ice.

"*Kosta, are you tryin' to scuttle us?*" shouted Nigel, manning the port oar.

Kosta pushed his oar against the floe. "*Then vlepo! I no to see it!*"

Andrew held onto the sheet, tightening and releasing it as the sail flapped in the fickle wind. The boats had been out of control since they'd hit the riptide. The men had tried to heave to, but the rudder had been useless against the storm.

The *Breen*'s sail was set. Siegal and Bailey were trying to coax the boat away from the berg.

"We can't get close this way!" Barth yelled. "I'm coming about!"

As the boat turned, Andrew released the sheet. The boom swung to port — but then it came back, as if losing confidence.

"She's not going over in this wind!" Andrew cried out.

"Fall off and try again!"

Barth turned the tiller again and Andrew yanked the sheet tight. The sail snapped outward against the force of the gale, and after a moment they tried the tack again. This time the boom cracked as it swung about.

"The boom is separating from the mast!" Robert shouted.

"Impossible!" Nigel replied. "I secured it myself."

Heeling hard to starboard, the boat picked up speed and began pulling alongside the *Samuel Breen*.

"*Tighter, Winslow!*" Barth said. *"We're going to collide!"*

The boat jerked as it struck something below the surface.

"*Ice!*" Lombardo yelled.

"*THIS IS INSA-A-A-ANE!*" wailed Oppenheim.

They were parallel to the *Breen* now. Separated by thirty feet at the most. Hayes leaned out over the

Breen's starboard gunwale, holding a stout line. *"CATCH THIS!"*

He flung the line hard. It soared through the air.

Robert reached out, his frame cantilevered over the sea. With his free hand, Andrew grabbed the back of Robert's coat and held tight.

The line splashed to the water, about three feet from Robert's outstretched fingers. He lurched forward.

His coat ripped.

Screaming, Robert tumbled over the hull. Andrew fell toward him, grasping desperately for some part of Robert, any part.

He got an ankle and held tight.

Robert reached up and held onto the gunwale. His fingers clung to the hull, his body skimming the surface of the water. The ice battered his shoulders and face, and he cried out.

Dr. Montfort leaned over the gunwale and took Robert's shoulder. "Heeeeeeave . . . *ho!*" Together Andrew and Dr. Montfort yanked Robert over the gunwale. All three sprawled into the bilges.

Robert coughed and gasped for air. "I — I'm fine. *Get the line!*"

The *Raina* and the *Breen* were pulling near.

Soon they'd be hull-to-hull. Hayes had pulled in the line and was waiting to throw again.

"*Look out!*" Bailey shouted.

Hayes threw. Andrew stood against the bulwark, arms open.

With an abrupt *snap*, the boom tore loose from the mast.

The sail blew out, ripping the sail sheet from its grommets. The boom smacked onto the deck and broke into pieces that clattered to the boat's floor.

Andrew fell back against the opposite gunwale.

Without any resistance to the wind, the boat quickly lost speed. The dogs, silent and cowering until now, began to wail.

"Hold the sail!" Captain Barth shouted. "Create some wind resistance and get us going — somehow. They're pulling away from us!"

"*O Captain, my Captain!*" Oppenheim cried out.

Robert grabbed Nigel by his collar and lifted him onto the deck. "You said you knew how to rig the boom!"

"I *fought* I did," Nigel said. "I mean, I might've been a mite *off* about the size of this bolt or that, I'm not perfick!"

Robert grabbed the sail. It flapped in his arms like a struggling child as he carefully isolated a corner. Sticking his finger through a grommet, he handed the other edge to Nigel. "Take this. Do as I do. We'll hold the sail as if *we're* the boom."

The two men struggled to pull the sail tight. It was an impossible task. The boat rocked uncertainly. The *Samuel Breen* was receding. *"Throw the line!"* Andrew called.

But Hayes had turned toward the iceberg. The men aboard the *Breen* were shouting, gesturing.

And bailing.

"They've hit!" Andrew shouted.

All hands on the *Breen* were bailing water over the bulwarks. The boat was stuck.

Nigel and Robert angled the sail tighter to the mast. The *Raina* picked up speed.

Andrew grabbed a piece of the shattered boom, then reached belowdecks and pulled a loose halyard out from underneath the dogs. He tied one end of the halyard to the mast and the other to the jagged block of wood, then stood up and yelled as loud as he could:

"CATCH THIS!"

Hayes looked up. Andrew reared back and flung the block high.

The wood hurtled toward the *Breen*, straight and true. Hayes caught it chest-high.

"Attaboy!" Lombardo cheered.

"Kalo to Theos!" Kosta exclaimed.

"I'm coming about!" Captain Barth yelled.

Nigel and Robert brought the sail around to port. The boat heeled awkwardly but slowly began to change direction.

The rope tightened. Andrew felt the *Raina* slowing down, pulled by the *Breen*.

The other boat was caught. The berg was holding her fast.

"Trim the sails!" Andrew said. "Pull harder!"

"We're trying!" Nigel retorted.

"The mast won't take their weight!" Barth shouted.

"Then I'll help it!" Andrew replied, grabbing onto the line.

"Andrew, you're going to capsize us!" Lombardo shouted. "They're not budging."

"What am I supposed to do, *cut her loose?*"

Andrew held fast. Eight men were on that boat. Eight men trying with all their strength to live. Siegal and Bailey were jamming oars into the water, trying to lift the *Breen* off whatever held it fast.

The *Raina's* keel was out of the water. She was listing hard to starboard. The men crowded to the uplifted port side, their heads now at least six feet higher than Andrew's.

"*Let go!*" Oppenheim cried out.

Andrew planted his feet against the inside of the starboard hull, now almost parallel to the water. He tensed his arms, threw his weight back, and pulled with all his strength.

Suddenly he fell back. The port side dropped.

Broken. It was broken.

The men of the *Breen* were goners.

Andrew sat up and glanced toward the berg.

The line hadn't sunk into the water. It stretched across the surface, still attached to the *Breen*.

Trying to tack, Nigel and Robert had lost control of the sail. The *Raina* had slowed — but the *Breen* was moving.

"HA! *You did it, my boy!*" Captain Barth whooped.

Andrew pulled. Lombardo grabbed hold of the line and helped him.

On the other end, Bailey and Nesbit pulled, too. The *Breen* slowly drew closer. Bucketfuls of water spilled over the side as the other men continued to bail.

"They're way below the waterline," Dr. Montfort said.

Nigel and Robert managed to find the right angle to the wind, and the *Raina* picked up speed.

In all the commotion, Andrew hadn't noticed where they were heading.

Toward Antarctica.

Andrew turned to Captain Barth. "We're going the wrong way."

"We have no choice," Captain Barth replied.

"But Jack said we had to —"

"We have no rigging. The *Breen* needs to be patched. We have to make land as soon as possible. If Jack were here, he'd do the same."

Andrew's leg began to throb again. His body shook.

If we separate, Jack had said, *if one boat is damaged — our return voyage is doomed.*

The team had split in half. Two of the four boats were crippled.

And those two were returning.

Andrew felt numb as the men began to shout anew and the dogs sent up a racket.

He turned and saw the *Samuel Breen* sinking beneath the ocean.

1 2

Jack

February 5, 1910

The ice was like stone.

It clung to the rigging, at least an inch thick. Jack tried to break it but he couldn't. The sheets were like solid pipes.

They'd set the sail, hoping to tack and return to the *Raina* and the *Samuel Breen*, but the storm had come up from nowhere. Now, rigid with ice, the sail was trapping the wind, making the boat heel and pitch violently.

Jack had to hold onto the mast for balance. The *Horace Putney* was veering crazily. "I need a hammer!"

Colin emerged from below the decking with an ax. "Use this, Father!"

Jack grabbed the hilt and smashed the back of the blade against the ice. *One . . . two . . . three . . .* A chunk broke off. Then another.

Mansfield pulled the sheet. The sail creaked. Jack pounded.

SNNAP!

With a sudden crash, the ice shattered like glass, and Jack jumped away. "Take 'er in!"

Colin released the sheet, lifted the boom, and lashed the sail. Cranston held tight to the tiller. Mansfield grabbed an oar and gave another to Philip.

"What do I do?" Philip asked.

"Row!" Mansfield replied. "You know how to *row*, don't you?"

"Indeed!" Philip dipped the oar into the water and tried to paddle.

"This isn't a canoe!" Mansfield shouted. "Use the oarlocks! Do what I'm doing. You hold while I back."

Philip inserted the oar into the lock and sat down. "Hold what?"

Jack took the oar. Submerging the blade, he

held fast while Mansfield backed the boat around to face the wind.

"I've lost sight of the *Iphigenia!*" Colin called out.

But Jack's attention was focused straight ahead. A swell rose on the horizon, spreading like a wide, sloping mountain. The *Horace Putney*'s bow pointed toward the center of it.

"Cranston, hold the rudder tight," Jack said. "We'll face this head-on."

The center of the swell bulged. At this distance it seemed to be standing still, although the water's roiling movement suggested great speed.

The wind caught the *Horace Putney* full blast, sending a spray of ice and spindrift into the men's faces.

"She's yawing!" Cranston cried out.

As the boat began to climb, the bow drifted south. Jack paddled furiously in the opposite direction. If she turned sideways to the swell, they were dead.

Up . . . up . . . up . . .

"Lord 'a' mercy!" Kennedy pleaded.

The men pitched forward to keep from falling back off the stern. Sanders screamed.

And then the boat crested.

For a moment the clouds stretched above and below them, as if they'd been jettisoned skyward and might now fly away.

But as the boat tilted down, the men were thrown backward, onto the deck with the yelping, frightened dogs.

Jack heard the creak of splitting wood.

The mast had cracked from the base clear up to the midpoint.

In front of them, the slope dropped into the clouds, with no bottom in sight. On the tiller, Cranston's knuckles were white.

They plummeted.

Jack took Colin's shoulder, and for a moment he thought of the scrawny little boy on the dock in Harwinton, Alaska, staring at the bay for hours waiting for Raina. And now he was a man, and the dream of seeing her again — both of their dreams — returned as the sea came to claim them.

The *Horace Putney* hit bottom hard, raising a wave that broke over the bow. The men scrambled for buckets and began to bail.

Jack glanced astern, looking for a shadow, any sign of life from the other boat.

All he saw was the black wall of water, receding in the fog.

The sea now lapped over the bulwarks, loaded down by the weight of the water. In the frenzy of bailing, no one spoke.

The mast was useless. Jack ran his hands along the crack and hoped that somewhere they had stored another mast.

A curtain of white emerged slowly to starboard. The shore was coming closer. "Colin, get the binoculars and find us a cove or a sturdy floe, someplace where we can put in and fix the mast. Mansfield, row us closer. Cranston, turn us forty-five degrees east of south."

As the three sprang into action, Philip grabbed an oar and readied himself to row.

Kennedy gestured for Philip to move aside. "I'll do it, Westfall."

"I'm perfectly capable of rowing," Philip said. "We do that in England, you know."

"Eyes to stern!" Sanders suddenly shouted. "They made it."

Jack turned. The *Iphigenia*, listing to port but intact, floated toward them out of the mist.

"Thank God," Jack said under his breath. He

pulled a rifle from under the deck and fired a shot into the air. Moments later the *Iphigenia* returned the signal.

Colin scanned the shore with the binoculars. "I see a cove."

Mansfield looked over his shoulder. "Where?"

Colin pointed out a small depression in the shoreline. "Beneath that long, jagged ridge."

Mansfield began pulling his oar harder. "Two o'clock, Philip!"

"Thank you," Philip replied. "How lovely to have a watch that works."

"That's not what I meant! I'm giving you directions. *Pretend* you're in the middle of a clock, got it? Now, straight ahead is twelve, behind you is six, to the right is three — "

"Right-o. Why didn't you say so in the first place?"

Philip pulled as hard as he could. And even though Mansfield's greater strength kept pulling the boat off course, they managed to gain quickly on the cove.

Colin was the first to notice the heads of floating seals — and the rocks. They made whitecaps in the waters of the cove, clusters of them all over the place.

"Oarsmen, take it slow," Jack said. "Cranston, point her toward the coast."

Colin had his eye on the port side. Jack focused on the starboard.

The rocks came up quickly, large and black. Volcanic debris. The boat was riding low, and the cloud cover made for shallow visibility.

Jack tried to keep a watchful eye, but the water was blurring.

His lids were heavy, so heavy.

He blinked. He shook his head hard.

Fatigue was out of the question. Alertness was all.

Eyes front. Focus.

Something was heading toward them, long and thick like a killer whale. And close.

"Pull it to port!" Jack shouted. *"To port!"*

The ship suddenly jumped.

A long, tearing sound ran from bow to stern.

The dogs leaped back, barking viciously.

"We're stove in!" Sanders shouted.

Jack felt the water gushing into the boat at his feet.

Part Four

Separation

1 3

Barth

"Walk! Move your legs!" Captain Barth tried to lift Hayes out of the water, but the man must have weighed 250.

"I — I — c-c —"

"Come on, Hayes, I was counting on you to *help* me!"

"C — co — cold —"

Barth pivoted around, knelt, dug his shoulder into Hayes's midsection, and stood. Hayes was draped over him like a sack of cornmeal.

Speed was crucial. Humans weren't supposed to survive in water like this for longer than ten minutes, fifteen at most. Hayes had been in for fifteen, Nesbit longer. Of the three dogs, Yiorgos had perished in the water. Socrates and Demosthenes had made the swim to the *Raina*. And they were both near death.

Barth was sure he'd lose all of the *Samuel Breen* crew. But they were sailors of the old school, scrappy and indestructible. Siegal and Petard had managed to climb on board the *Raina*; Bailey, Brillman, and Stimson had grabbed onto her gunwale and hung on as they sailed to this godforsaken floe. The others — Hayes and Nesbit — had swum all the way.

Or tried to. Hayes had made it to within twenty feet before he seized up. Nesbit was still in the water.

Robert ran to the water. "I'll get 'im, Captain."

"N-n-no, all h-hands are needed in the infirm-m-mary." Barth shook uncontrollably as he deposited Hayes carefully on the tarp. "Hayes is alm-most gone, M-M-Montfort. You've got a j-j-job cut out for you."

"Captain . . . ?" Robert said.

Barth ran back to the edge of the floe. It was insane to risk Robert on this.

Nesbit was out maybe fifty yards. He was a good swimmer. But he wasn't even trying.

Barth jumped into the water. Contact felt like

a gunshot. Fishing Hayes out of the water hadn't prepared him for total immersion.

He faded in and out of consciousness, swimming hard. He had no feeling below the waist and could only hope his arm motions would jump-start his system. When the arms started to spasm, he prayed he was kicking.

"Nes . . . bit!"

The blue in Nesbit's eyes seemed to have run out, leaving only white.

And then he was under.

Barth dived. The water was clear but dark. Nesbit was a black blur.

He reached desperately and grabbed hold of something. Fabric.

He pulled and the black blob came with him. He thrust himself back to the surface and lifted Nesbit's head abovewater.

Nesbit convulsed. A thick stream of water and saliva spewed from his mouth.

The floe seemed miles away. Lombardo and Robert were standing at the edge, shouting.

How far was it, really? Fifty yards was a child's distance. He'd been trained to pull a flailing victim four times as far.

Forty yards.

Nesbit was heavy. Deadweight. Dead weight. *Live* weight. He was alive. He couldn't die. Not on Barth's watch.

Thirty.

This was all his watch, wasn't it? This was his expedition — number 137 for Elias Barth, United States Navy captain, retired. At large. For hire. No commitments. No family.

Only friends.

Friends were those in whose company you thrived. To whom you dreaded bidding farewell.

Twenty.

The sea was his friend. The *Mystery*.

Nesbit.

These men.

The black ice.

Ten.

Farewell.

1 4

Colin

February 5, 1910

"Nice vacation spot," Kennedy said.

Ruskey threw open his arms. "I name this paradise Elysium!"

"That's where the ancient Greeks went after they died," Philip remarked. "Their idea of heaven."

"I feel sorry for them," Flummerfelt said.

Dismal was too kind a word to describe this place. The shore was a patch of rocks, salt-washed and slickened with guano and seal excrement. The wind shrieked from all directions, a downdraft from the ice cliff that encircled them like a fortress wall.

Even the dogs, restless and dazed from the voyage, had no scamper in their souls.

Where a section of the wall had collapsed, a steep, gravelly path led farther inland. But no one was particularly interested in exploring.

The *Iphigenia* was intact, resting in the westernmost part of the cove. The *Horace Putney*'s hole was big but reparable. And Flummerfelt had located a sturdy spar in one of the boats, large enough for a new mast.

They were lucky.

Colin hoped the other boats had been, too. He kept his eye out to sea, hoping for their appearance any minute. Everyone suspected the worst, so no one dared speak about them.

As Kennedy sawed wood, O'Malley fired up a Primus stove to boil seal's blood.

There would be no shortage of that. The bay was dotted with the domes of a few dozen seals, distinguishable from the rocks because their heads bobbed.

"Aw, no!" Kennedy threw down his saw in disgust and gestured toward the water. "Look!"

Cranston gasped in mock horror. "It's an ocean! And here I thought I was back on Lake Ronkonkoma!"

"The tide is coming in, you fools!" Kennedy shouted. "We must have pulled in at dead low."

The joking stopped.

No one had noticed any high-tide line here. It was one of the first things a sailor looked for on a beach, a telltale strip of seaweed and detritus high up the beach that marked the farthest edge of the tide. If no line existed, you assumed you'd arrived *at* high tide.

But because algae and fish were so sparse here, the line wasn't easy to spot. Now Colin saw it, a slight but definite darkening at the base of the cliff.

Which meant that in a few hours the entire cove would be underwater.

"Come on, let's lift her up the path," Mansfield said.

The men tipped the *Putney* upright and threw in the tools, wood, and stove. When they were done, they spaced themselves around the boat, Father to Colin's left and Philip to his right. "Heave . . . ho-o-o-o!" Jack called out.

It wasn't as heavy as Colin had expected.

"Hey, easy there on port!" called Rivera from the other side. "You don't know your own strength, kid."

"Sorry!" Philip exclaimed.

"Not you," Windham said. "*Colin.*"

As the men walked carefully across the slippery

rocks, Dr. Riesman yelled from above: "There's a ridge up here! A cave, too."

The footing was treacherous over the loose rocks. At Father's command, the men turned and began climbing sideways to the incline, for stability. Sanders and Rivera each tumbled once, almost upsetting the balance. Philip fell twice to little effect.

Talmadge and Dr. Riesman met them at a long plateau, about ten feet wide, that looked like a kind of fault line between two halves of the ice cliff.

As they set the boat down, Colin eyed the cave. It was triangular and deep, rent between two slanted, massive ice formations.

Rivera was already heading for it. "I'll scout out the lodgings."

"What for?" snapped Kennedy.

"Shelter," Rivera replied. "Warmth. We may need it."

"We're settin' up a guest house here?" Kennedy asked.

"Wyman, please . . ." Father said.

"We're going to unstep this mast, slap on a new one, and put in, and it ain't going to take *that* long," Kennedy said. "I was raised on a farm — we worked until the job was done."

"Kennedy, you'll love it in here!" Rivera called out from the cave mouth. "It smells like a barn."

"Oh, do save me a spot," Philip murmured.

"If we need to, we can always turn these babies upside down and use 'em as shelters," Kennedy said. "Side by side, the *Putney* and the *Iphigenia*'ll be at least the size of a twenty-man tent."

The *Iphigenia*.

Colin ran toward the path. He heard the crunch of running footsteps behind him. At the top of the incline he glanced down into the cove. The wind had picked up, raising six-foot breakers on the shore.

The tide was half in, and the *Iphigenia* was no longer on solid ground. Tethered to a vertically protruding rock, it pitched fiercely on the water.

Colin descended fast. The boat wasn't far out yet.

"*Colin, watch it!*" Father called from behind him.

Colin skidded to a stop. His feet went out from under him and he fell.

A wave rose out of the churning surf. It towered over Colin ten, fifteen feet and opened like a black-gloved hand.

He turned and scudded back across the stones. Father grabbed his hand and pulled him back to the pathway. The other men waited, halfway up.

The wave crashed behind him, and he felt the sting of freezing water on his back.

As they joined the men, Colin and his father turned.

On the backwash of the wave, the *Iphigenia* rose fast. It left the surface for a moment, pausing in the air, and flipped. Another wave slammed into it, thrusting it toward the rocks.

It smashed into pieces, jettisoning wood far out into the sea.

The crashing surf sounded like laughter.

15

Andrew

February 7, 1910

Andrew watched the *Raina* float away, carrying four men. Robert and Nigel pulled hard at the oars against the brash. Behind them sat Petard. The body lay out of sight, wrapped in a tarp under the decking.

When the oars stopped their rhythmic plunging and the boat began to slow, Andrew turned away. He heard a soft but substantial splash, a brief prayer.

When he looked back, the *Raina* was coming about. Petard now held an empty tarp.

The sea had claimed the first victim of the *Samuel Breen* and the *Raina*.

Nesbit had been a powerful presence. Like Shreve, he was steady and keenly intelligent. Unlike Shreve, he was cautious. He thought ahead.

Sometimes even those qualities didn't help.

Nesbit had never regained consciousness in the two days since Captain Barth's rescue. He'd remained in a coma until this evening, when his breathing finally stopped.

Dr. Montfort, who had been standing by Andrew, now turned silently and slumped into the tent. He had to care for his other patients.

Barth would be next to go, most likely. He had neither moved nor spoken in two days. Hayes, at least, could moan and ask for water.

Demosthenes and Socrates still lay nearly motionless. It wouldn't be long for them, either.

At the edge of the floe, the three sailors climbed out. Silently they pulled the *Raina* onto the ice, then disappeared into the other tent.

Andrew curled up in a tarp by the tent flap, his position for night watch. The wind blew off the Ross Sea, picking up moisture that intensified the cold until it could penetrate fabric, limb, and organ, until it congealed the marrow in Andrew's bones. The sun now made a brief nightly disappearance below the horizon, and the fact of darkness was frightening.

Soon the Antarctic summer would be over. In two months, the dark would begin to overtake the light until it swallowed up the entire winter season.

Andrew hated night watch. Hope was the first thing to go when you were alone. It was in short enough supply anyway.

The name of their present home, Camp Hope, had been Andrew's idea. He thought it would help raise morale. Morale was as important as food.

The trek inland — in*ice* was more accurate — had been awful. None of the men had fully recovered from the disaster at sea.

They'd managed to drag the *Raina* along the ice and snow to a more solid floe. It still didn't seem as stable as it should — you could feel the motion of the current — but the men were in no condition to travel farther.

No one had yet addressed the issue of returning. Survival had taken all the energy the team could muster.

But now, with the men snoring and the dogs whimpering in their sleep and the night reaching in, Andrew could think of nothing else.

The *Raina* could only be rowed now, but Robert had begun repairs on the rigging, along with a team made up of the fully recovered men. They'd all dutifully followed his instructions — including Nigel. After the incident with the boom, Nigel had had the good sense not to contradict anyone on anything.

And yet the question remained: What happened *after* the boat was repaired? They couldn't all fit in. Did they all stay here to die, out of fairness? Or did they draw lots — home for the winners, death for the losers?

There would be fights. The men would tear one another apart.

And what about the ones who did leave? What were the odds of sailing to safety over nearly 3,000 miles of treacherous freezing seas, with no food and little shelter, in a jury-rigged rowboat?

Andrew tried to stop the thoughts. He gazed out over the water, hoping for the thousandth time to see the silhouettes of the *Horace Putney* and the *Iphigenia*.

He heard a rustling behind him and turned. Oppenheim was awake, crawling toward the tent flap. Andrew dreaded this. The babble would be unbearable without anyone else awake to soften the blows.

But Oppenheim sat quietly next to Andrew and pulled his canvas blanket around him. "They're coming," he said.

In the dusky sky over the sea, the light began to change, its hidden particles of color gathering as a cloud gathers from vapor. They blazed and faded in a diaphanous shimmer of purple, blue, and red, as if a curtain were being slowly drawn across heaven. In the water Andrew saw dancing shapes that transformed into hideous sea monsters, sinking ships, flailing men. He saw Nesbit reaching up, his face bone white. He heard Dr. Shreve's voice explode in a desperate cry that slowly receded, and the shrill wail of dogs about to die on the ice. He heard Jack and Colin calling for him, asking him to come along. And Mother, singing out his name.

He felt caught in the moment between death and life, looking forward and backward at the same time.

Faith, hope, and love — these ideas had sustained him on the South Pole trip. But it was different then. Then he was returning to a ship, a family, the idea of going home.

Now he had none of the three.

Without a word, Oppenheim slipped away and went back to sleep.

Over the water, the aurora australis winked and faded.

16

Jack

February 7, 1910

"Mansfield, how long's it gonna take you to step that mast?" Kennedy barked. "An' *what*, pray tell, are you doin' with that seal's blood, Westfall — paintin' a still life? Smear it on, boy!"

Kennedy, who'd never been known for patience and flexibility, was losing what little he had of each. The repair to the *Horace Putney* hadn't been minor at all. In sawing the wood around the hole to make a neater fit for the new planks, the hull had caved in. The wood had dry rot. It had probably been rotting for months, escaping notice back in New York. And in repairing *that*,

Kennedy had discovered "structural flaws" in the boat, things that could prevent it from sailing true.

Jack hadn't understood a word of his explanation, but you didn't contradict Kennedy on matters of carpentry or design.

They had worked straight through, taking shifts. Some of the men had slept in the cave, despite the darkness and the atrocious stink. Others had taken shelter under the overturned boat, managing to sleep soundly despite the noise of repairs. Kennedy had been awake for at least seventy-two hours.

"She should be ready to sail in a few hours, as soon as the caulk sets," Dr. Riesman said.

Jack shook his head. "We'll leave her overnight. We need rest, all of us — especially the ones sailing back."

Flummerfelt peeked out from the starboard side, where he was helping sand down the hull. "You got that right."

"I could sleep like a hedgehog hidin' in the canebrakes," Kennedy murmured.

"He's human after all," Ruppenthal grumbled.

Kennedy whirled around and grabbed Ruppenthal by the collar. "Repeat that?"

"At ease, gentlemen!" Jack said, pulling them apart.

They would need the cave. No doubt about it. Without shelter, without a sense of a home base, the men would be at one another's throats.

He'd have to explore. Despite the smell.

"Who has the matches?" Jack asked.

"I do," Colin said.

"Come with me to the cave and bring a lamp."

Colin reached under the decking and pulled out a small kerosene lamp. "Sorry, Kennedy, I won't be gone long."

"I won't miss you," Kennedy replied. "Stumble-bum — Flusterfield — whatever your name is — up here on the double."

Colin climbed down from the boat and walked with Jack toward the cave. "Who's going? Tomorrow. With you."

"You are," Jack replied. "Only one other. We need speed and flexibility."

"Who's the other?"

"Philip."

Colin gave him a tenuous look.

"I'm serious."

"But *why*?"

"I can't leave him here, Colin. The men'll make mincemeat out of him."

"Father . . ."

Colin fell silent. He couldn't argue that.

The smell of organic waste came out to greet them from the cave opening. Colin covered his nose. Jack reached into his pocket and pulled out Walden's flag to use as a handkerchief.

The rocks outside the opening were smooth and slick, like the ones below, no doubt from centuries of seal visitations. Among them, Jack saw three tiny white slivers.

Burned matches.

"Who left those?" he asked.

Colin shrugged. "Not me."

"Has anyone else been using the matches?"

"Nope. I've had 'em since we left Camp Perseverance. Robert has the only others, and he's on the *Raina*."

Jack picked one up. It was whole.

Matches were priceless. Only a half box remained. Jack had strictly ordered the men to use them only if absolutely necessary — and to cut them in half, to double their lives.

"Looks as if someone's hiding something from us," Jack said.

"But why?" Colin asked. "Why keep something like that secret when it could help us all?"

"As we get further into this mess, Colin, I understand more about how to manage men but less about their motives."

Colin pulled out his pocketknife. He took a match and laid it on a flat rock. With a firm but delicate stroke he sliced the match in half, taking care not to crumble the head.

As Jack cupped his hand around it, Colin struck the match and quickly ignited the blubber in the lamp. Crouching in the cave entrance, he held it forward.

The light played dimly against the smooth walls of ice. Shadows formed by long icicles danced a hoedown. The floor was cluttered with odd-shaped objects.

"Bones," Jack murmured.

"It's the seals' chophouse and mausoleum," Colin said.

"The seals' outhouse is more like it," Jack remarked. "Let's clean it."

"The shovel was in the *Iphigenia*."

"We'll use oars then."

"You dropped something." Colin knelt to pick

something off the ground. He held out a small American flag to Jack.

Jack took his hand away from his mouth. "I didn't drop it."

"Then . . . where'd this come from?"

Jack held his flag side by side with the other.

They were identical.

17

Andrew

February 8, 1910

"Hey, fellas, the old man's alive!" Lombardo shouted.

He and Petard had been saying daily prayers by Captain Barth's side. Apparently they'd been answered.

The men crowded into the makeshift infirmary. Barth was turning his head slowly. "I'm not *old*, you nitwit," he mumbled.

"Yeeee-HAAAAH!" Lombardo cried out.

"How are you feeling?" Dr. Montfort asked.

"Dandy," Barth drawled. "Just prop me up and point me to the banquet table."

"Hungry!" Oppenheim threw his head back and laughed. "Imagine that. As if he's the only one starving here."

"Oppenheim, have some respect," Lombardo snapped.

"Respect for what?" Oppenheim replied. "Barth? If he'd had a lick of sense he'd have died and decreased the surplus population."

"Enough, you blaspheming lunatic!"

"Sticks and stones may break my bones — and no one cares but Davy Jones!"

Lombardo bolted upward from his crouch, and Oppenheim darted out of the tent.

"You better run if you know what's good for you!" Lombardo bellowed.

"If you stopped acting like a gorilla, sailor," Captain Barth said, "people wouldn't bait you. Thank you for your prayers. Dismissed. All of you!"

"Thank *you*, sir." Lombardo stood, bowed, and backed out of the tent.

The sailors were moved by Barth's survival. As they filed out, Andrew could feel the change in the air. A spark of optimism.

Dr. Montfort brought Barth a mug of freshwater, melted from snow.

"How is Nesbit?" Barth asked.

Andrew glanced at the doctor, who shook his head slowly.

Barth's eyes grew suddenly glassy. "Did he suffer?"

"He never woke up," Dr. Montfort said.

"He was one of the best." Barth looked away. "Hayes?"

"He's right behind me, Captain. Recovering. Exposure and frostbite. He'll be all right, I think."

"And the stores — any meat?"

"The men are hunting. The seals seem to have migrated. Unfortunately we'll have to be patient."

More than patient, Andrew thought. Soon they'd have to suck nutrients out of wool.

The men had been hunting daily. So far they'd brought back two penguins, a skua, and an albatross. Not nearly enough meat.

Seals and penguins were sustenance out here.

The camp would have to be moved closer to the wildlife. But who knew where the wildlife had gone?

Andrew's stomach was beyond painful. It felt dried out, shriveled and hard like a walnut. Today his tongue began to water at the sight of the dogs. The thought horrified him. But once, the thought of eating seals and penguins had horrified him, too.

Hunger warped your mind. You saw the world in two categories, *edible* or *inedible*. And the definitions changed daily. How far down the evolutionary chain could you slide before you completely lost your humanity?

The hunters would return soon. Maybe today they'd be lucky.

Andrew stood to leave. "Good to have you back, Captain."

Barth nodded impatiently. "Yes."

As Andrew hobbled out, he leaned on a cane made of a plank from the *Mystery*'s deck. Its handle resembled a comely young woman — whittling courtesy of Brillman.

Outside the tent, he placed weight on the injured leg. It still hurt like the devil — maybe a little better than the day before, but not much.

"Oppenheim, get up or I'll throw you out."

Lombardo again. Inside his tent now.

"Who's going to force me?" Oppenheim asked.

"You want to see force? I'll show you force!"

Stimson rushed toward the tent. "Get 'im!"

"Fight!" Bailey shouted.

Andrew made his way to the tent. Inside, Lombardo and Oppenheim stood on opposite sides of a cot. Lombardo's fists were clenched, his face red.

"Lombardo, you're going to give yourself another heart attack!" Andrew called out.

"He was lying on my cot when I got in here," Lombardo exclaimed. "He knows I'm sick."

"I'm sick, too!" Oppenheim said. "Everybody says so! Why should you get the deluxe suite, you bombastic lickspittle?"

Lombardo stepped over the cot. "*I'll kill you. I will personally take you apart, do you hear me?*"

"Do it, Vincent. Please. Kill me. Then kill everybody else. Do us all a favor, will you? Because if you don't, the cold will. Or the water. Or the starvation."

Lombardo had Oppenheim by the throat. "*You want me to do it! YOU REALLY WANT ME TO DO IT, YOU WHINING, GOOD-FOR-NOTHING —*"

"Stop it!" Andrew shouted. He grabbed Lombardo by the arm and tried to yank him away.

The cane fell. Andrew tumbled to the ground and howled with pain. It felt as if the wound had been ripped open.

Stimson and Bailey stooped to pick him up. Andrew struggled to his feet.

The men had pulled Lombardo off Oppenheim now, but he was still seething.

"Oppenheim, come with me," Andrew said, taking his cane.

"Me?" Oppenheim asked. "Where are we going?"

"For . . . a walk. I need someone to . . . spot me." Andrew took his arm and ushered him out the tent flap.

"You're lucky, Oppenheim, do you hear me?" Lombardo shouted. "Next time I see you, you won't be so lucky!"

18

Philip

February 9, 1910

"We're tacking!" Jack shouted. "Ready about!"

"Tacking, yes," Philip said. "Tacking . . ."

The sail suddenly swung around like a gate. The large horizontal block of wood hurtled toward Philip's cranium.

With a shriek, he ducked.

Duck was what they meant to say. *Duck.* Why were these sailors so obtuse?

And why, out of all the men left behind on that dark satanic shore — all professional sailors of great distinction — was Philip chosen for this trip?

They wanted to kill him. That was the only plausible explanation.

The recent catastrophe had affected their minds. Perhaps that hideous cave contained noxious gases. Winslow and son had indeed become a bit strange after cleaning it out — wan and morose, as if they'd discovered the remains of some long-lost relative.

The boat was turning hard, rising up on one side. Philip clutched the edge to keep from falling.

"Father, it's sucking us in," Colin said.

"Sucking?" Philip squeaked.

"Hold on tight, Philip!" Jack warned.

Philip looked over his shoulder. He wished he hadn't. He wished he'd had the sense to curl up under the deck and cower.

The boat was at the edge of a maelstrom, a whirlpool of such viciousness that it sloped downward like the open maw of a malevolent underwater creature.

"Get us out of here!" Philip shouted. "Tack . . . or something!"

The two Winslows fussed with the sail, pulling and changing angles, but it did no good.

"Stop, Colin!" Jack cried out. "It's no use! Slacken it!"

"You're not giving up, are you?" Philip asked.

"No!" Colin loosened the sheets and the sail

went slack. "Once we're in the pool, the sail does more harm than good. It'll make us heel!"

The *Horace Putney* was in the pool, all right. She tilted toward the center, gaining speed. Philip's sight blurred. The water's deafening rush sounded like a massive industrial machine.

He could no longer hear Jack's or Colin's voices, but he could see them both on the tilted foredeck, struggling to stay upright. The sail's bottom edge was blowing in the breeze, the wooden thing — the boom? — flailing wildly against the shins of both men.

That wouldn't do. Philip slid forward. Fighting dizziness and nausea, he clutched the boom and held fast.

Colin gave up trying to lash the sail. He grabbed the mast with one hand, his father with the other. They were yelling something to Philip, but he couldn't hear them.

The mast bent with Colin's weight. Philip pushed the boom aside and reached up toward him.

With a *crrrrack* that resounded even over the surging waters, the mast split.

Colin vaulted off the deck, over Philip's head, and into the boat, pulling Jack with him.

Philip cringed, covering his head with his hands. He heard a thud.

When he looked up, Colin was leaning over his father's inert body, listening for breath, shaking him.

He was out cold. Dead, perhaps.

One down, two to go.

Philip closed his eyes. This was it, wasn't it? This was why God had spared him when he'd fallen through the ice. A quick demise wouldn't be proper for a wretch like Philip Westfall, would it? Better a slow, cruel death spinning in an ever-quickening gyre. . . .

"*I STOLE THE MONEY!*" Philip cried out, casting his eyes heavenward. "*I DID IT, BUT I WAS PUT UP TO IT BY THE OTHERS! OUR GUNS WERE TOYS — TOYS, DO YOU HEAR? I WILL TAKE FULL RESPONSIBILITY AND REPENT! TAKE ME, DELIVER ME FROM THIS PLACE, BUT AT LEAST SPARE COLIN AND HIS FATHER!*"

Philip felt himself sobbing.

He sounded ridiculous.

Fortunately Colin hadn't heard a word of it. He was trying to stanch a wound on his father's head with a wet strip of cloth he'd ripped from his own coat.

The boat was still miraculously afloat. If Philip wasn't mistaken, the whirlpool was flattening, too. Losing a bit of strength.

Philip snatched up two oars from the boat floor. He jammed them in the oarlocks.

And he rowed.

1 9

Andrew

Exquisite.

In his dream, Andrew is in a restaurant and it is exquisite. Mother sits across the table. She looks young and beautiful, the pneumonia long gone, not the trace of a care on her face. The warmth of her eyes could melt away the entire Antarctic ice cap. And perhaps it has. The other two places at the table, set for Colin and Jack, are empty. But they're coming, too. Very soon.

Outside the window the fog is thick. It seems as though they're floating on a cloud. And perhaps they are. Andrew is bursting to tell Mother about the menu, but he doesn't have to. Right then the waiter arrives with two dinners. He's a funny sort of fellow, wearing white tie and tails and waddling in an odd manner. With great pomp and dash, he raises the two plates over his head, then sets them on the table in front of Andrew and Mother.

On each plate is penguin meat.

Mother's face goes white. She is appalled.

Andrew, however, is ravenous. He picks up his knife and fork, plunges them down, and

KKKRRRROKKKKK!

"What was that?"

"I don't know."

Hayes. Petard.

Andrew opened his eyes and sat up. The dream fell away in fragments.

Around him, the men were waking. The noise had been real.

The taste of penguin remained in Andrew's mouth, and he ran his tongue along his still-greasy lip. He felt the pleasant bulge in his belly and remembered the sight of the animal slow-roasting over a pit.

Then the memory of the previous night rushed

in. The walk with Oppenheim. A sudden chittering noise behind a pressure ridge. A frozen pond full of penguins. A slaughter.

He felt like throwing up.

What had happened? What had he become? An animal. All instinct.

And it had satisfied him. Afterward, back at camp, the smell of roasting meat had brought tears to his eyes and made him drool. His reaction had been no different from that of Socrates.

It was happening just the way he feared it would. A person was an animal, a person had to eat.

Brillman headed for the tent flap. "Probably some pressure ridge tipping over."

"Not near the infirmary, I hope," Stimson said.

"Don't worry, we'd hear Oppenheim complain," Siegal remarked.

Brillman's eyes were locked on something outside. He blanched. "Oh my lord. Get out here, men. On the double!"

The sailors pulled on their jackets and raced outside.

Andrew forced himself up, using the tent post for support. The men were racing toward the jagged edge of a narrow stream.

"What is it?" Captain Barth called from the infirmary tent.

"The floe is splitting, sir!" Andrew called back.

"What direction?"

"West."

"Then strike camp and move southward while we're still attached!"

The crack was growing around to the south now. The floe pitched on the current, twisting away from the ice sheet.

Robert began taking down tents. Nigel gathered up supplies. Holding Demosthenes in his arms, Kosta whistled for the other dogs. Brillman and Siegal turned the *Raina* right-side up, and then Dr. Montfort and Petard loaded aboard the injured, in their cots. Except Barth. He insisted on walking.

Bailey and Stimson crowded all the supplies around and under the cots, and the camp was ready to go.

Andrew joined the men as they gathered around the *Raina*. He could support himself on the ship's bulwark and even lend a little muscle to the push.

"Ready? Ho-o-o!" he shouted.

No one snickered. No one balked at listening to him.

They all pushed forward. Southward. Farther into the ice cap.

Behind them was a sound like the snap of a great oak tree.

Andrew glanced over his shoulder and saw what was once Camp Hope break into small chunks that bobbed slowly out to sea.

2 0

Philip

February 9, 1910

Pull.

Philip felt nothing.

Pull.

His gloves were rigid with ice. His blisters had grown, burst, bled, then given way to new blisters underneath, which had grown, burst, and bled. His backside chafed against the motion of rowing, and he sat in a moving pool of blood. Saltwater clung to his skin through every item of clothing.

Pull.

Since the maelstrom had ceased — by an act of a merciful God or blind luck — the coast and the sea had remained indistinguishable in the fog. Colin and Philip were in constant motion, but it seemed they hadn't moved a centimeter. Their oars had grown heavy with encrusted ice, but they didn't dare stop to break it off for fear of collapsing.

Pull.

In the shadow under the decking, Jack shifted positions.

Philip unlocked his frozen jaw and spoke. "Conscious?"

"No," Colin replied.

Pull.

Pull.

"Colin?"

"Mm."

"Why are we doing this?"

"Doing what?"

"Going back."

Pull.

"Why do you think, Philip?"

"If they survived, don't you think they'd have kept on sailing?"

"Yes."

"Then they would have found us."

"Maybe."

Pull.

"Don't you agree?" Philip insisted.

"Well, what happened to *us*?"

"Us?"

"Mast damage. Hull damage."

"Ah."

Pull.

"We put in," Colin said.

"Yes."

"Maybe they did, too. Somewhere else. Another cove."

"Perhaps."

Pull.

"You think they're dead, Philip?"

"Or rescued. That Walpole fellow."

"Walden."

"Walden. He may have found them. Perhaps he's coming back to get us."

Pull.

Pull.

"That would be lovely, wouldn't it, Colin?"

* * *

Pull.

"They . . . weren't," Colin said.

"Pardon?"

"Rescued. They weren't rescued."

"Oh?"

"He's gone. Walden."

"What do you mean, *gone?*"

Pull.

"I mean, he's already sailed through here."

"How do you know?"

"We found his flag in the cave. Matches. A cigarette. Human waste."

"Are you sure they were his?"

"Can you suggest any other possibilities?"

Pull.

"And that's why you and your father were so . . . inscrutable?"

"Sorry."

"You *knew?* You knew we were doomed *and you didn't say anything?*"

"We thought it would bring down morale."

Pull.

Philip was stupefied.

The plan had hinged on Walden. The alternative, Defection Island or whatever that bloody place was called, was ludicrous. Even with the *Mystery* it would be an outside shot.

Pull.

Philip felt everything now — the friction, the blisters, the sores, the pain. The excruciating, *senseless* pain. The realization that every moment, from his humiliating arrival in New York to this slow boat to oblivion, had been the piling on of calamity upon catastrophe that led to only one possible conclusion.

Pull.

"Then why pretend there's hope of rescue?" Philip demanded. "Why row, Colin?"

"Because."

"What kind of fool reason is that?"

"Because there is never — *never* — a good reason to stop trying your hardest."

Pull.

"Oh, that's rich, Colin. Lovely. Bloody inspirational. Well, let me try to think of a reason. Ah, *I* know: We're three thousand nautical miles from anyplace where Weddell seal is *not* considered a rare delicacy, our whereabouts are known only to one wretched human being who fouled our cave and sailed off — and, if we're very lucky, we number thirty men and thirteen dogs *in three rowboats!* *There's your reason!*"

Pull.

"Why are you laughing?"

"To hide the fact that I want to cry!"

Splash.

"Philip?"

"What?"

"That noise? Did you hear it?"

"What noise?"

"The splash!"

"I hear nothing *but* splashes. Is this some sort of game? Shall we count them, then? Onetwothree-fourfive —"

Thump.

Philip shut up.

"Did you feel that, Philip?"

"Of course I did! What is it?"

"I don't know!"

They stopped rowing.

And slowly, on its own, the *Horace Putney* started to move. Sideways.

"Colin, something's underneath us!"

"I'll get the gun —"

Colin ducked under the decking. His father stirred and opened his eyes.

From the port side came a deep watery bellow like the sudden release of a thousand fire hoses.

Philip was afraid to turn and witness the thing that was now reflected in the eyes of both Colin and his father.

As he peeked slowly over his shoulder, he saw the flank of a humpback whale submerge, and the beast's tail slap the surface of the water like a gun-shot.

Part Five

Desperation

2 1

Jack

February 9, 1910

"It must think we're a fish!" Colin shouted.

"It doesn't *think*!" Philip shouted. "It's a beast. It destroys!"

Jack stood at the bow. The fall onto the gunwale had raised a bloody welt on his head, and it throbbed. His bandage was wet and sticky, and his brain felt three sizes too large.

He held the broken mast waist-high, waiting for the whale to emerge. If he struck it, it might turn away from the boat and leave them alone. Or it might be angered into fighting back.

Which?

In an emergency you asked the right question.

Every problem yielded somehow. But a whale was different.

A whale decided your fate.

No cleverness, strength, or skill prepared you for its attack. Its victims littered the seafloor. With a shift of its bulk, it could break the hull of a five-masted whaling vessel containing two-score crew. Melville called it the Leviathan, a sea monster conquerable only by God.

The *Horace Putney* didn't stand a chance.

Colin rowed with powerful strokes, trying to direct the boat away from the beast.

It was thrashing, kicking up its tail as if the boat had poisoned the water. A plume rose from its back. Water rained down in thick, putrid drops.

Philip sat staring at it, his oar still.

"*Row, Philip!*" Colin shouted.

The boy was paralyzed. Laying down the mast, Jack took up the oar. He shoved Philip aside and plunged it into the surf.

"It's . . . bleeding," Philip said.

"It must have scraped itself on the hull!" Jack replied.

"No wonder it's angry!" Colin shouted.

"No," Philip said. "That's not why. It has something in its side."

Jack glanced over his shoulder. "What is it?"

"A harpoon," Philip said.

"How can it have a harpoon out here in the middle of —"

Colin was cut off by a high, screaming sound. A long object burst through the clouds.

TTHHHHWUCK!

Jack stopped rowing. "What the —?"

As the whale dived underwater, it rolled over. One long metal spear pierced its flank, another jutted from below its blowhole.

"Father!" Colin cried out.

"You see?" Philip said, leaping to his feet. *"We're saved! Ho, there! Whalermen!"*

"Sit down!" Colin admonished.

SHHHHINNNG!

Another harpoon whizzed over the deck of the *Horace Putney*, narrowly missing Philip.

Philip dropped to the deck. "Just call me Moby."

"They don't see us!" Jack exclaimed.

"We can't survive this far to be speared like animals!" Philip shrieked.

Colin crawled under the deck and came back with a hurricane lamp, filled with seal blubber.

Jack pulled the box of matches from his pocket. Only two left. No time to cut these in half.

165

He cupped his hand around the match. Colin put a hand overhead as an umbrella. Jack struck the match and held it to the wick.

It blew out.

One left.

"Philip, help!" Jack commanded.

Philip removed his coat. He huddled with Colin and Jack, holding the coat over their heads.

Light. Please. Please, Lord, don't let this blow out.

He struck again. The match flared.

A gust of wind sneaked under the coat, and the flame blew sideways.

Colin and Philip squeezed closer to Jack, blocking the wind.

Jack thrust the flickering match into the lamp.

It went out again.

But slowly, the seal blubber began to glow. As Colin slammed down the glass housing, the flame rose. And danced.

Colin held it high.

"*H-O-O-O-O-O-O!*" the three bellowed.

The whale rose again from the depths. Closer now.

TTHHHHHWUCK!

A fourth harpoon grazed its side, opening a

long gash. Blood sprayed into the foam. The whale was enraged, desperate. Like a stuck bull, it snorted and heaved its bulk high into the air.

It crashed down beside the *Horace Putney*, sending up a tremendous wake.

The boat's port side lifted upward. Jack, Colin, and Philip fell to starboard. The lamp flew out of Colin's hand and into the sea.

All three grabbed onto the boat's frame and held on as the whale slammed against the keel, shattering it. Jack felt his fingers slip. He heard Philip shriek. He turned to look for his son, but his back hit the water and he sank fast.

He tried to swim upward but the shock immobilized him. He saw pieces of boat fall around him in slow motion.

Colin. Where was Colin?

He kicked. He swept his arms down to his side and rose. He thought of the word *shock* — quick, percussive — it really wasn't like that, was it? It overwhelmed you head to toe then

gradually took away

all

your

energy.

Jack burst above the surface. The two boys were alive. Next to him. They were young. They had a fighting chance. Maybe.

He tried to say good-bye but he had no strength.

Through his heavy eyelids he saw a gargantuan gray shadow come toward them out of the fog.

2 2

Nigel

February 9, 1910

Nigel was at the end of the tie-line — the last person of the team, pushing the stern of the *Raina* over the ice.

It was the worst place to be when every man's stomach jittered like a pricked balloon on account of severe gas pains brought about by hunger.

The snow blew in his face so hard that it left pockmarks on his goggles. The wind felt as if it were scraping his cheeks to the bone. His fingers, because they no longer had meat on them, chafed inside thick gloves. His sweat tasted funny, like a medicine, which anyone knew was a sign your body was breaking down. The ice under his boots still looked thin, which meant the team had a long way to go. There wasn't a seal or penguin in sight. Nigel's stomach was convulsing.

And on top of all of it was the *smell*.

It was a bloody torture of all five senses.

"Gen'l'men, kindly refrain from coupin' le fromage, if you catch me driftwood," Nigel said. "It breaks me consecration."

"Drift," Siegal corrected.

"Concentration," muttered Robert.

"I don't care *wha'* you call it!" Nigel shot back. "Drift, concentration, crepitation, flatus, cheese cuttin', wind breakin', gas warfare — *a fart's a fart. Now just stop it.*"

One or two of the traitors were laughing. It took a lot to laugh while you were face into a blizzard, pushing a loaded boat across old, bumpy ice. It took a bloody good joke.

Nigel was not joking.

Everyone was sick. Brillman had scurvy. Probably Oppenheim and Petard, too. Nigel had seen it happen to a hundred sailors. It was nothing a little warmth, relaxation, and fresh lemons couldn't cure.

They were dead men.

Nigel was a dead man. And Andrew and Barth

and the entire crew. None of them wanted to say it, but they couldn't stop him from thinking it. It was lunatic to be moving *into* the ice. Even the mightiest seagoing fleet with a crew of thousands could never actually find them here. The idea that they could have met Slappy — or whatever that American mapmaker was called — was absurd. And as for the other two boats — well, if they'd been able to return, they would have. Jack would have seen to it.

They were dead, too.

Dead, dead, dead, dead, dead, dead.

The snow fell like bullets now. The wind screeched, mocking them, mocking their clothing — informing them, Sorry, they'd overstayed their welcome and must be eliminated.

Barth was calling out. "Stay together! I can't see you — count off!"

Nigel called out his name along with the others, but his voice no longer came from himself. It came from another man, a blighter he'd once known, a fool who had the dunderheaded idea to hide in the storage hold of a barquentine for what he figured would be room, board, and a little adventure.

That man was fading away.

Soon Nigel's fingers slipped from the boat and his legs stopped.

Someone called to him but he didn't move. His tie-line, slack at first, grew taut.

The roar came at him like a solid thing, louder than the wind. He'd never heard it before, but he knew what it was. He had expected to find it here eventually. No one believed him. Lucky souls. It only sought out the ones who believed.

Now Nigel felt five sharp pulls on his line. Come along.

He reached into his trouser pocket, pulled out his pocketknife, and cut himself loose.

He was free.

The yeti summoned. You could resist its call, they said. But you always gave in.

The howl came from all directions but he knew its source. He walked into the blizzard — but he felt his body growing slowly warmer. Such was its power, they said. It drew heat from the cold and flesh from ice. They said.

After a long time he came upon footsteps, large footsteps. As he followed, the snow blew over the prints. In a moment no one would be able to tell a soul had been there.

The footsteps circled around the side of a ridge. They ended at the mouth of a cave.

The roar beckoned. The beast would be satisfied.

Nigel walked into the cave.

The snow rushed in behind him.

2 3

Colin

February 9, 1910

Blind.

He was blind. He couldn't see a thing, couldn't feel (*the whale, where was the whale?*) because the water was hungry; first it sucked the heat from him and then it went after his life. "F — fahh — ther!" he cried out. "Ah — I ca — nn't —"

The darkness lifted. He saw shadows, foam. Whitecaps. Two shapes.

Philip, flailing.

Father, going under.

His fingers closed around his father's shirt and he pulled.

Philip tried to swim toward them. He was blue.

His eyes were strangely wide and luminous, as if the lids had been peeled away. Reaching out weakly, he too tried to hold up Father.

"S-Save . . . yourselves," Father said.

"W-We do this t-together, Father." Saltwater rushed into Colin's mouth. He was sinking, losing his senses. "Ph — ilip?"

"Yes."

"Thanks."

"For —?"

"S-Saving our lives. For . . . rowing out of . . . the m-m-maelstrom."

There. Colin had owed him that.

Behind Philip's head, the gray shape loomed toward them.

Colin felt no fear. It was time.

He prayed silently that the water would take them before the whale did. That they would be claimed by the sea, the way Mother had been claimed.

But the shape was gaining steadily.

As the fog rolled aside, Colin saw it clearly.

It was not a whale.

It was a prow.

"C-Colin . . . ?" Philip coughed.

A good high one, fanning back to outline a broad beam.

The hull was encrusted with barnacles and smeared with blood. Five stout square-rigged masts emerged from the fog, interlaced with staysails. Attached to the ship's bowsprit was a figurehead, a wooden statue of a mermaid. Two towering metal winches hunched over gunwales laden with long rowboats, racks of spears, and harpoons. Along the bow, peeling gold-and-green letters spelled out the name NOBADEER.

A whaling ship, full-tilt after a catch.

"H-H-Help —" Philip sputtered.

Colin tried to cry out, but his voice was frozen.

The ship's crew stood at the port bow, facing away from Colin and Philip, searching the seas ahead. As the bow cut swiftly through the water, it smashed through the floating remnants of the *Horace Putney*.

The water closed around Colin like a fist (*why, Lord*) and he realized he would die within hailing distance of a ship that by all odds shouldn't be here, and whose disappearance meant the certain death of the entire expedition.

"W-W-W —" Father said.

"What?"

"WAVE!"

Colin raised an arm limply. The beam of the *Nobadeer* glided past them now, sending a powerful wake.

"C-Col — lin —" Philip said. "Look. Up."

As they rose on the wake, Colin saw over the starboard gunwale. The men were swarming the masts, pulling at halyards, slackening the sails.

The ship was losing speed.

One by one, sailors in striped shirts gathered at the port rail like sparrows on a telephone wire. They waved and pointed, shouting incoherently.

A lifeboat began to swing, and then it slowly descended. Over the side peered two men, goggle-eyed with surprise, as if having suddenly come upon flamingos. One had a robust red beard and the other was clean-shaven and craggy-faced. Both were enormous fellows, burly and well fed. Colin had forgotten that men could be that big.

"*Ahoy! Cavortin' with the merpeople, are ye?*" called Red Beard.

"Oh, no, a Br — Briton!" Philip's eyes rolled upward and he sank.

The lifeboat splashed down. The men immediately rowed toward Philip with powerful synchronized strokes.

177

"Up ye go, matey!" Crag Face reached into the water, fished out Philip, and plopped him roughly in the boat. "All right, the old man next!"

Father was too weak to reach upward.

"Didn't eat our sausage this morning, did we?" Red Face said, yanking Father on board, and then Colin.

Colin fell to the floor of the ship. Father was immobile but breathing. Philip was blue.

"Shall we take the lift, Mr. Harkness?" asked Crag Face.

"Yes, indeed, Mr. Bardsley," Red Beard answered.

They hung onto Colin's words and asked him to repeat himself constantly. They interrupted his tale with shouts of "Garn!" and "Bloody 'ell!" and "Good God!" and other more colorful phrases that made even Colin blush.

The sailors' quarters, the fo'c'sle, was small and warm and cramped, and it stank of fish and whale meat. Colin felt he could live here forever.

Father was sitting on a wooden stool, sipping strong tea. He wore a black wool watch cap on his head and two thick blankets around his torso and legs. His feet were nestled in a metal pail of hot water.

Philip lay passed out on a cot.

"So, let me 'ear ye straight," Harkness said. "Y'say the mutiny come *after* the return of the South Pole team —"

"And then the ship sunk," Bardsley added, "and then come the trek across ice — and the whirl-pool —"

Colin could hardly believe the story himself. It had the pace and the outlandishness of an oft-told fairy tale, and he felt as if he were back home, out-side the school, trading stories with his friends. He sipped his tea and tried not to burst out laughing. "Yes. Then Philip rowed us out — somehow — all by himself. He saved our lives."

"Just in time for the whale," Bardsley said.

"And the rescue by yours trulies," Harkness added.

"But yer shipmates is stranded in some cove south-by-southwest," Bardsley said, "and 'alf yer crew's back in the Ross Sea, if they're still alive."

"Yes," Colin said, lifting the cup to his lips.

"And if you could help," Father said, "we'd be sure the United States government found out about your deed."

They were silent. Staring at Father uncompre-hendingly.

"Yer ain't serious, are ye?" asked Bardsley.

"Ye're pulling our leg," said another sailor. "Like, maybe ye was just out 'ere a-fishin'?"

Harkness exploded with laughter, sending a spray of Assam tea across the room.

A good part of it landed on Philip. He woke up with a start. "Oh! Oh bloody yes, take me already! How many times must I put up with these confessions —"

Philip blinked. He swallowed his words and looked around, the tea dripping off his brow and onto his lips. "Oh. Hello. Is it teatime?"

Bardsley belched a laugh. And now all the sailors joined in, doubling over, slapping one another's backs, snorting and spitting and stomping their feet until Colin began to worry about the decking.

"I have seen the underworld," Philip murmured, "and it looks and smells like a fo'c'sle."

"Ye three ain't exac'ly gardenias yerselves," Bardsley grumbled.

"Colin 'ere tells us you're a 'ero," Harkness said, wiping his brow.

"You're — British, aren't you?" Philip said.

"*English*," Harkness said proudly. "Me accent give it away?"

"Do you . . . happen to *know* who I am?"

Harkness leaned in. The laughter had died down and now every man joined in examining Philip's face.

"Yeah . . . " Harkness said, his eyes widening. "Yeah!"

Philip moaned. "Oh, I knew it . . ."

"Blimey, lads!" Harkness slapped his forehead. "We were supposed to bag us a *whale*. And 'ere we go pickin' up the *Prince* of Wales!"

"Hooo-haaahahah!" Bardsley bellowed, setting off another round of laughter.

"*WHO LET THE MONKEYS ON THE SHIP?*"

The voice cut through the noise.

All laughter ceased. Polished black leather boots stomped down onto the ladder, followed by a cape made of thick, boiled wool with a brocaded edge. A golden scabbard clanked loudly on silk breeches as the man descended.

At bottom he turned to face the men. He resembled an old pirate king, still stuck in the nineteenth century. His eyes were coal-black, floating in the shadow of a heavy brow, and a long mane of silver-black hair streamed thickly beneath a beaver-skin hat. His nose's journey from forehead to lip had been detoured at least three times, and a long scar under his right eye locked a permanent lopsided grimace onto his face.

"Beggin' your pardon, Cap'n —" Bardsley said.

"Silence!" the man shouted, his eyes fixed on Jack. "I be Coffin. Captain Rhadamanthus Increase Coffin."

"Jack Winslow," Father said without flinching. "My son, Colin, and Master Philip Westfall."

"A deep pleasure, I'm sure, Your Highness," Philip said. "Er, Holiness — *Captaincy* —"

"They're in fine workin' order now, Cap'n," Bardsley insisted. "Able seamen, all three. But y'see, there's just a few more of 'em a-stranded on a cove not very far from 'ere at all —"

"You nattering chowderhead, more crew means more sailors to pay!" Captain Coffin thundered.

"Exac'ly wha' we told 'em, Cap'n," Harkness quickly said. "No pickin' up strangers wha' are starvin' in coves. Cap'n Coffin wou'n't allow it, no, sir — we knew we could speak f'yer, Cap'n, seein' as we knows yer mind —"

Liar.

Colin bolted up from his seat, but Jack held him back.

Captain Coffin shot Harkness a look that could

slice steel, then turned back to Jack. "I can't pay ye but an eight hundredth lay — a thousandth each to the boys — but don't let me hear ye complain. Y'oughter be grateful 'tain't nothing!"

"Fine!" Philip blurted out. "Quite reasonable indeed."

"Have ye a bath and a shave, ye look like somethin' wha' escaped the madhouse." Coffin turned away, his cape billowing out. "Now, Harkness, let's bag us a whale or two — and on the Sabbath day, ye'll set us on a course to find those other men!"

As the Captain stomped abovedecks, Harkness gave Colin a smile and wink.

24

Andrew

February 10, 1910

This is how it ended.

Silent and shivering under a miserable icy overhang that barely protects you from the wind, a leeward pressure ridge to extend your life just a bit longer.

Not with a heroic fight, a stirring speech, a pledge of "courage to the death!," a noble tableau at final curtain.

It just ended. Without dignity, redemption, or flair.

One man dropped away without a word. Then another.

You went through the motions of trying to find

the missing. Because knowing was better than not knowing. But you knew they wouldn't be found. They were gone. And you envied them.

Andrew held tight to a guy wire and reeled it in. The wire had been tied to another and another, and finally to the entire length of line in their possession.

On the other end, Petard and Stimson were out looking for Nigel and Captain Barth.

The captain should have traveled on a cot in the boat. He should have been resting, not leading the trek. But he believed in heroics. He thought he could set an example and stir the troops.

He hadn't been ready. In the thick of the storm he'd lost his way for reasons unknown. His line had snapped and the blowing snow had been too thick for anyone to find him.

Petard and Stimson had been out for an hour before they'd given Andrew the signal — five tight pulls — and now they were headed back.

As the wire curled at Andrew's feet, he heard Lombardo snoring from beneath the *Raina*. Along with the tents, the men were using the upended boat as a shelter. No one spoke of repairs anymore. And no one bothered to come out and keep Andrew company.

Soon Petard's and Stimson's shapes emerged from the blizzard, slumped and slow-moving. Ice clung to their beards like tusks, and their eyes drooped with exhaustion and disappointment.

"Nothing," Stimson said.

Barth was dead. And Nigel. But Andrew felt no grief. He felt no emotion at all.

Petard knelt and began to pray softly. "The Lord is my shepherd, I shall not want . . ."

As if by signal, the other men filed out of the tents and gathered in a circle. Petard looked out toward the bleak landscape as he spoke.

" . . . Yea, though I walk through the valley of the shadow of death, I will fear no evil: for thou art with me; thy rod and thy staff they comfort . . ."

His words trailed off.

Poor Petard. Even he, the spiritual rock, was torn apart by this. Andrew put a comforting hand on his shoulder.

But Petard was staring intently into the storm.

A hulking shape moved toward them, a misshapen creature grotesquely thick around the shoulders.

Andrew remembered talk about the yeti. Nigel was convinced that it existed somewhere in Antarctica.

Silly, superstitious talk.

"What on earth is that?" Andrew murmured.

The creature staggered to a stop.

"Don't just stand there, you blithering imbeciles!" it cried.

"Nigel?" Petard said.

The men ran toward him. As Andrew came closer he realized why he hadn't recognized the profile. Nigel had something on his shoulders.

"Take this, will you?" Nigel said, slipping Captain Barth down into the snow. "You find the strangest things in them blasted caves."

25

Ruskey

February 13, 1910

Sanders looked skeletal. The sun had made deep pools of his cheeks and eyes. Behind him, O'Malley brought up fragments of the *Iphigenia* that had washed up on shore. His jacket was cinched around his waist, which was the size of a thigh. The caption cried out: Slow Death on Two Feet.

Snap.

Three shots left now. Last roll.

"Will you put that thing down?" Kennedy said. "You're gettin' on my nerves."

The vest-pocket camera was junk, really. He missed his big Hasselblad, with its capacity for huge panoramas, its aperture and shutter-speed settings that allowed for resolution down to the individual grains of snow. But alas, no blank plates, no Hassel-blad. Everything lost in the wreck of the *Iphigenia*.

Couldn't agonize over spilled plates. Had to keep on.

The little camera did have its virtues. It caught candid, day-to-day life. People. Motion. Progress. It would be a record of what went on here.

Besides, it kept him busy.

And sane.

Sanity was precious. Already some of the men were cracking. O'Malley had tried to make soup out of snow, wood, and stones. (He had a theory about edible algae and sloughed-off seal nutrients. But the soup had tasted like wood and stones.) Talmadge was taking weather readings by the minute, record-ing the tiniest changes in temperature. Ruppenthal was picking fights. Cranston was writing notes in his journal, ripping them out, and tucking them into rocks in the cave. Kennedy had lost his sarcastic sense of humor. That was scariest of all.

Hunger had changed them all, turned them into scavengers. It was a constant companion, tear-ing at their insides until they thought of nothing else. It made walking cadavers of once-burly men.

It made good photography.

189

Windham, on lookout shift, had dug himself a deep, full-body indentation in the cliff, banking the sides to protect himself against the wind. But he had fallen asleep there, standing up, his soot-blackened face turned to the sun. His lips, thin and parched, had curled back over his teeth, and he looked like an Egyptian mummy unearthed in its sarcophagus.

Pharaoh of the Frozen South.

Snap.

Two shots left.

Rivera, pacing a figure eight, his footsteps wearing a path in the gravel. Dr. Riesman's eyes, feral and desolate, peering from the shadow of the cave.

Eternity's Limbo.

Frame, angle, composition.

Snap.

One left. Last shot.

It would have to be good. The best.

Ruskey began to shake.

He thought of the sign he'd painted over his studio door back home, the dying words of the poet Goethe: *More light*.

Light was life. It illuminated and nourished. If light died, life ended.

He imagined his finger pressing the shutter, the

final image imprinting itself on the silver nitrate, the aperture snapping shut for good. Forever.

The camera vibrated as Ruskey lifted it to his eyes.

He couldn't do it.

He couldn't not do it.

If someone ever found this place, they would need to know what happened. They would see. And if they saw, they'd know. They had to know.

One shot left. No blanks aloud.

Take it while you're able.

He slowly panned, taking it all in: men, boat, cliff, pathway, rocks, shore, sea, ship . . .

Ship?

He blinked.

It was impossible.

2 6

Andrew

February 27, 1910

"'Scatter, as from an unextinguished hearth/ Ashes and sparks, my words among mankind!/Be through my lips to unawakened earth — '" Andrew glanced up from his book. His voice was killing him.

Only Oppenheim was listening. Most of the men sat listlessly on the ice. Captain Barth stood, scanning the landscape with a spyglass.

The sight of Barth still amazed Andrew. The fact that he was alive — that he'd been found and rescued by Nigel, of all people — was a miracle. It had lifted camp spirits tremendously.

But most of the positive energy had dimmed the day after the rescue, when the sun finally emerged.

It revealed that the men had not trekked inland at all. They'd gone in a semicircle, more or less parallel to the ice's edge.

During the days since then, the camp had remained under the same pressure ridge while Barth recovered. The experience had changed him and Nigel. Neither would talk about what had happened, why they'd wandered from the boat, why Nigel had cut his line. Both seemed quiet, frail, haunted.

The weather had turned warmer over the weeks — summer's last gasp — and the ice edge had crept steadily closer. But no one had the energy to move camp inland. For that you needed real food, not a diet of melted snow, an occasional bird, and on some glorious days a lost penguin or seal.

Soon moving would be inevitable. Until it became so, Andrew had been determined to pass the time reading aloud. To introduce beauty into this bleak, most unpoetic of places.

"Come on, finish!" Oppenheim blurted out. "'The trumpet of a prophecy! O Wind,/If Winter comes, can Spring be far behind?'"

Andrew smiled. "You know that poem."

"'Ode to the West Wind,' Percy Bysshe Shelley," Oppenheim replied. "All my students had to learn it."

"Those poor kids. Ain't you guys got any songs?" Lombardo said. He twisted his lips into a strange sideways shape and honked, "'Ohhh, my w-i-i-ife's a corrrker, she's a New Yorrrker, I give her everything that moneeeey can buy —'"

"Roowooooooo!" squalled Socrates from inside the boat tent.

"*Stamàteh, vre!*" Kosta scolded.

"'She's go-o-ot a pair of le-e-egs just li-i-ike two powder kegs — uh-ohhh, that's whar my money go-o-oes!'"

"Knock it off, Lombardo!" Captain Barth shouted.

"I got a thousand more," Lombardo said.

"Well, swallow the other nine hundred ninety-nine," Nigel snapped, "and let us perish in peace."

Lombardo shrugged. Andrew closed his book. Nigel returned to his gloom.

Back to normal. No motion, no voice. No wasted energy.

The noise, for a moment, had felt good.

Captain Barth put down his spyglass and walked back to the tents. His face was gaunt and hooded, his beard scraggly and thin. He looked like an old, old man.

"Thanks, Winslow," he said softly. "I liked that poem."

"I got a thousand more," Andrew said.

"We need one about moving. About picking up and moving camp when nobody cares."

"Just give the order, Captain."

Barth nodded wanly, as if to say, *Fat chance*. The fire in his eyes was out. The incident in the snow, Andrew realized, had done that. Being put in the position of having to be saved by Nigel was a defeat, a humiliation — a reminder that he had been unable to save Nesbit. To Barth, these were two failures in a life that didn't permit such things.

Andrew knew the feeling.

From the boat tent came a soft, keening sob. Kosta's. Another dog had starved to death. Demosthenes, most likely. They were down to five now: Socrates, Iosif, Nikola, Panagiotis, and Kristina.

To the east, a loud crack resounded. The ice was breaking not far from them. Captain Barth stiffened.

Another crack. To the west.

Andrew felt the floe shudder.

"Up!" Captain Barth said. "On the double, men, we're moving out!"

A few of the men looked up. Robert, Petard, and Dr. Montfort stood.

"I mean it — *move!*" Barth tried again.

No one budged.

Barth turned to Andrew, his eyes the color of fear.

"What's going on?" Andrew shouted. "You're all just giving up?"

Brillman shrugged. "In the end, the land always wins."

"Victory to Antarctica," Bailey muttered.

"Victory to the bottom of the world," Siegal grumbled.

"To the bottom," Lombardo added.

CCRRRRAACKKKK!

Andrew fell backward. The ice had split.

The dogs ran out, baying at the sudden change.

The men, one by one, sat in a rough circle, shoulder to shoulder. All except Captain Barth.

Andrew understood their action. Herd instinct. They were animals, gathering in some primal, communal death impulse. The land always won.

He fought to see. He fought to think.

Instincts:

Fight.

Hunt.

Defend.

Attack.

Ideas:

Plan.

Foresee.

Outwit.

Prevent.

No. No. No. No. No. No. No. No.

Tried. Failed. All.

Something. There must be something. Every crisis yielded to the right question. Jack always said that.

But what? What to do? The basic questions didn't hold anymore. Andrew had asked them all. He had run out.

What would Colin do?

Andrew took a deep breath. His vision cleared.

He looked out at the ice. He saw a dark spot on the horizon.

Quickly he gathered up whatever wood he could find. Then he ducked into the boat tent.

He grabbed a match.

2 7

Jack

February 27, 1910

Jack didn't recognize it at all. None of the land-
marks were there. The entire geography of the Ross
Sea had changed in a month.

"'Ave ye seen it yet, aye?" called the second
mate, a crusty harpooner named Henry Fee who had
just emerged from the deckhouse.

Jack shook his head as he continued slowly to
scan the horizon through the ship's binoculars. The
location of Camp Perseverance was anybody's guess.

His feet were numb from standing on the crosstrees for such a long time. At first the whalers had
gathered below him, cheering him on, enjoying the

excitement and the break in routine. But now most had wandered off to their various chores. Even the dogs — Maria, Ireni, Stavros, Martha, Kalliope, Fotis — had lost interest.

Besides Fee, only Harkness, Colin, Mansfield, and Philip remained.

"Not meanin' t'be rude or nothin'," Fee continued. "Just in the manner of warnin', mind ye — but ye been up thar a long time, and the Cap'n'll be expectin' ye to bear fruit, else we must needs shove off, on account o' time bein' money, and it's a sure bet the whales be a-grinnin' at their great good luck —"

"Will ye pull in yer scroll, Mister Fee?" Harkness interrupted. "I can't 'ear meself think."

"Nothin' *to* 'ear, 'n' that's a common fact!" Fee retorted.

"We're jibing hard to southeast," Colin reminded him. "Our position changes by the minute."

"The angles open up, the pressure ridges reveal hidden places," Mansfield added. "We can't stop until we sail the entire sea."

"Exactly," Philip said, "and if your charming leader can't understand that, he's not worth the water he tacks through."

"I'll tell the Cap'n you said such," Fee snapped.

"Tell him it is our humble request," Jack called down. He looked sharply at Philip. They were guests. With a man like Coffin, you remembered your place.

Colin and Mansfield were right to ask for more time. What they hadn't said was that the ship had nearly traversed the whole sea already. The sailors were keeping the *Nobadeer* at a safe distance, not wanting to be stuck in brash or worse.

And if you allowed yourself to think about it, to use logic and sense, you realized this was a fool's errand. In the end, after the effort was made, the right and compassionate thing to do was face the truth and turn back.

Now the Ross Sea's eastern shelf loomed off the starboard bow. It would soon be time.

Jack whispered a good-bye to Andrew, and in the binoculars' orbs saw a dream image of a frightened little boy who'd hid when Jack was courting his mother. Who'd cried through the wedding and the move to New York, refusing to call him Father even though his own father never spoke to him. Who, when things overwhelmed him, would lose himself in literature, adventure stories, and poetry. Who'd faced his mother's death with flint and courage. Who'd conquered the Antarctic to save a man's life and had never given himself credit.

The image of the boy faded, and Jack saw nothing clearly. The enormity of his mistake settled thickly over him. Half his crew — his own stepson — lost. Not one soul besides Horace Putney aware of his location. His own life — Colin's, Philip's, and the other men's — saved only at fortune's whim, a chance crossing in a stormy sea.

He had failed to reach the South Pole. He had failed to exercise a plan of rescue. He had failed in his one ironclad promise, the safe return of his crew. He had failed at being a leader, a father, a husband. And he would pay for it the rest of his life.

His hands shook.

"Father?" Colin said. "Are you all right?"

"Still looking," Jack replied.

Through the lenses now he saw only a cloudy whiteness, a distant flock of penguins resting on a small ice floe, all blurred by his tears and split by the glare of the sun.

It was time.

He blinked the tears away.

The glare remained.

And it undulated.

It rose upward and vanished in wisps of white and gray against the blue sky.

Jack adjusted the binoculars, teasing them out to the absolute highest magnification.

It wasn't glare at all.

"Colin," he said. "Colin, get up here."

"What do you see?"

"Just get up here!"

Colin was up the mast in seconds.

"What do *you* see?" Jack asked.

Colin took the binoculars and trained them at the horizon. "Smoke? *Father, it's smoke!*"

"Someone had to make that smoke, Colin — and it wasn't those penguins!"

"Those aren't penguins."

Jack grabbed the glasses away. The dots on the floating disk of ice were moving in a jerky fashion, jumping. Beside them was a small rectangular object from which more dots emerged. The smoke rose from their midst.

"It's them!" Jack shouted. *"Those are my men!"*

"I'll be a whale's 'ump," Harkness said.

"Yeeeeee-hahhhhh!" Mansfield lifted Philip off the deck.

Jack and Colin scrambled down from the crosstrees and followed Harkness, who was running toward the deckhouse. "Cap'n! Cap'n, sir!"

He flung open the deckhouse door. Captain Coffin sat at a small table, counting money from a weather-beaten wooden chest. "Harkness, you beslubbering clotpole! Ye made me lose count."

The news had spread instantly, and now both crews, Jack's and the *Nobadeer*'s, gathered around the door, yammering with excitement. The dogs wound their ways among the forest of legs, yipping bewilderedly.

"Beggin' yer pardon, Cap'n," Harkness said, "but Winslow 'ere 'as sighted 'is men, 'n' they us, it appears!"

"Yes?"

"So with yer permission," Harkness went on, "I'll give the order to set sail to the southeast until we're close enough to reach 'em by rowboat!"

"Are ye daft or deaf, mate?" Captain Coffin said. "I've already given me order to come about. We be a-runnin' half a hemisphere behind schedule, with contracts to fill, men to pay — and by now them dastardly beasts is flappin' their tails in our gen'ral direction, larfin' out their blowholes."

"But my son is on that ice!" Jack protested. "You can't do this!"

Coffin turned back to his money. "I can, on my ship. Dismissed, the lot o' yer."

Jack wanted to kill him. But Harkness grabbed him firmly by the arm and whispered, "Not now."

"Let me at 'im!" Kennedy shouted.

"Don't bother. We'll turn the ship ourselves!" Mansfield declared.

"Ha!" Fee laughed. "Ye'll be walkin' the plank afore ye can lock eyes on a staysail."

All the men shoved forward, shouting, their words jumbling together:

"'E's the devil, 'e is!"

"Aw, Cap'n, 'ave a 'eart."

"Nay, mate, the Cap'n speaks for the good of the *Nobadeer* 'n' its men!"

"Think on it, if it be yer own son!"

"'E ain't got no son nor wife. What manner of woman'd 'ave 'im?"

Harkness shoved two fingers in his mouth and let out a piercing whistle. "Quiet, mates!"

"Thank ye, Mr. Harkness," Captain Coffin said dryly, riffling through his money.

"Cap'n Coffin's a *whalin'* man — no more, no less!" Harkness said. "Think ye that the importers 'n' traders care if 'e leaves a dozen landlubbers to die on the ice? Nay, lads, they're whalin' men, too. They weighs the blubber and pays the tab, thank ye kindly. And if ye thinks men like that'd *cheer* a cap'n for the rescue of 'uman bein's, if ye thinks they'd praise 'im and spread 'is fame from port to port, Nantucket to the Azores, thereby perhaps raisin' the cash value of 'is catch —"

Captain Coffin glanced up.

" — well, then, ye don't know whalin' men, do ye? When they finds out the cap'n turned 'is taffrail to the only starvin' wretches on the entire godfor-saken continent, leavin' 'em to shout 'Please rescue us, don't let us die!' afore they wither to a lonely, needless end — why, they'll praise the name of Cap-tain Rhadamanthus Coffin for choosin' the want of a whale over the lives of 'is fellowmen."

"Aye!" Coffin's eyes were murderous. He stood, resting his fists on his table. "Aye, I'm a whalin' man, all right. But ye have a lesson to l'arn in the ways of godliness, Harkness."

"Why, Cap'n," Harkness said, "I was merely givin' the men yer own account of the matter, thereby savin' ye the odious task —"

"I can handle me own odorous accounts," Cap-tain Coffin snapped. "And I know whalin' men a far

205

sight better'n ye do. *Trim the sails and we'll head southeast, men! We won't leave here without those wretches! Dismissed!"*

Smack. Harkness pulled the deckhouse door shut with a barely disguised smile of triumph. "'E's a bit eccentric."

The men raced to the deck, hollering and praising the name Harkness.

As Jack climbed the mast again with Colin, the crew bellowed a raucous sea chantey.

Jack stood on the crosstrees and held the binoculars steadily.

Twelve . . . thirteen . . . fourteen.

"I count fourteen men," Jack said. "Some dogs, too. They have a tent. They made one of the lifeboats into a shelter — I don't see the other one."

"There were *fifteen*, Father," Colin said.

Jack couldn't make out any of the men's faces, but their silhouettes were sharpening. "Hayes. No mistaking him. There's Robert. Nigel, I think —"

"Is he all right?"

"Nigel? I believe so —"

"My brother! Is my brother alive?"

Jack nearly dropped the binoculars.

He felt himself lighten. He had to hold extra tight to the mast for fear he'd float away.

The figure who'd been stoking the fire elbowed his way through the group and began waving furiously.

Jack didn't need to see the face. He could recognize Andrew's shape a thousand miles away.

He gave Colin the binoculars. "Here, son, see for yourself."

2 8

Andrew

February 27, 1910

"*Here!*" Andrew shouted. "*We're here!*"

"They *know* we're 'ere, you fool!" Nigel shrieked. "'*ERE!*"

Tears ran down Oppenheim's cheeks. "It's not a mirage, it's not a mirage, it's not a mirage, oh, Lord, it's not a mirage."

Rowf-rowwf-roooooooowwww! howled Socrates and his pack.

"Praise God, from whom all blessings flow . . ." Petard murmured.

"*My Lo-o-ord, what a mornin'*," Lombardo sang. "*When the su-u-un begi-i-ins to shi-i-ine!*"

Nigel was dancing a Scottish reel, pulling Robert

208

along with him. Kosta was on his knees holding up a bewildered Panagiotis, doing a Greek dance.

"Ee-hah!" Dr. Montfort shouted.

"A little more from the diaphragm, doctor," Captain Barth said.

"*YEEEEEEEEHAAAAAAAAAAAAH!*"

"Now, that's a *sailor*!"

A whaling ship. It wasn't Chappy Walden's barque, it was a *whaling* ship. How did it get here? What was it doing so close to Antarctica? Where was Walden?

What did it matter? They could have come on the backs of mermaids for all Andrew cared.

The ship had hove to, and now a lifeboat was heading their way through the brash and pudding ice. As it approached, Andrew could make out the people on board.

He didn't recognize the barrel-chested sailor with the bushy red beard. But he knew the other two.

He nearly ran off the ice to greet them. They were alive. Alive and waving and smiling!

"*Colin!*" he shouted. "*Father!*"

"Avast, sailor!" Jack shouted.

When they bumped up against the shore, all Andrew had to do was open his arms. Colin and

Jack leaped off the boat and wrapped him fore and aft with an embrace that smothered and crushed and utterly exhilarated him.

"You're all right! You're all right!" Colin said over and over, his words high-pitched and soupy with emotion.

Jack yanked Andrew loose and swung him around until his feet left the ground, exactly the way he'd done it when Andrew was a child.

And as soon as he was set down, Andrew felt himself rising again — this time *with* Colin and Jack — lifted by Siegal and Petard and Brillman and Stimson and Bailey and Hayes and Dr. Montfort and Lombardo and Kosta and Robert and Nigel and Oppenheim and Captain Barth. All of them with a strength and assurance that their depleted bodies had reserved just for this occasion.

"They flyyyy through the air with the greatest of eeeease," Lombardo sang. *"Those daring young Winslows upon the high seeeeeas . . ."*

They danced — holding the Winslows aloft to that bleat of a voice — until Kosta yelled *"Hasà-piko!"* and they were on the ice again, arm in arm, following Kosta as he leaped and gyrated despite his toeless feet, in a gravity-defying dance that could have gone on all day.

Harkness climbed on shore, shaking his head. "Barmy," he said. "Completely barmy."

Andrew, Colin, and Jack dropped their arms. They looked at one another silently, then at the whaler.

"Ohhh, no, ye don't," said Harkness, backing toward the boat.

Andrew yanked him into line, into the dance, against his bitter protests.

Part Six

Home

2 9

Colin

"Mum," Philip whispered. "Oh, Mum . . ."

The woman on the dock looked like Philip. She was trim and a bit slouched, in the way of People Who Owned Things. Her dress was dark green and of a conservative cut, and beneath her fashionably tilted hat was a stubborn but mournful smile.

She saw Philip and waved, a cupped hand swiveling demurely from side to side.

"She's overwhelmed," Philip said, sniffling.

The London harbor was all noise and motion, sailors hauling sacks over the wooden docks, gap-toothed vendors hawking meat pies and bread, pubs shaking with the noise of laughter and chantey-

215

singing. Beyond the port, the streets trailed off into the fog, in narrow curves lined with tidy brick buildings.

It was a brand of madness at once more chaotic and more inviting than the cold, brutish docks of New York.

The *Nobadeer* was equipped with a radio, and Captain Coffin had sent word of the ship's arrival. A dock had been cleared, and two steam tugboats had puttered out to greet them. Coffin intended to stay as briefly as possible.

"Now get yer carcasses outa here as soon's we set the plank," Captain Coffin growled. "Ye've already a-wasted me time enough so's I can kiss away a decent two months' profits."

"Yes, it was delightful for us, too," Philip said.

"What about the money you promised us — a thousandth lay, was it?" Colin said.

"It's questions like that'll nip a promisin' young life in the bud," the captain replied.

The crew of the *Nobadeer* swarmed over the deck, letting out the halyards, racing up into the rigging, and furling the sails for a smooth docking. Colin admired their skill. A five-masted square-rigged vessel   now that was a challenge. Someday it would be fun to sail one.

One by one the men of the *Mystery* gathered by the bulwark. Colin felt his father's left arm on his shoulder. "Shreve would have loved this scene."

"As would Nesbit," Captain Barth said, gripping the gunwale.

"We'll have to inform their next of kin," Andrew suggested.

"What will we tell them?" Colin asked.

"That two good men gave their lives in the highest pursuit of their calling," Captain Barth replied softly.

"Look at them all," Lombardo said, shaking his head in amazement. "It looks so easy, don't it — life?"

Mansfield's eyes were misty. "I don't know if I'm ready for it."

"Strange," Petard said, "it scares me more than that iceberg did."

"Nothing will ever be the same," Dr. Riesman said. "Working a job, going to the market, falling asleep at night — how can anything seem important after what we've seen?"

"And what we've conquered," said Sanders.

"Conquered what?" Kennedy grumbled. "It conquered us."

"No," Colin said gently. "You're wrong about that."

"We survived," Ruskey reminded him. "That's a victory."

"Because of *luck*, that's all," Kennedy said.

"Is it luck for one man to hope when the rest have given up?" Captain Barth asked, looking pointedly at Andrew.

"For a landlubber to row a boat out of a maelstrom?" Colin said.

"For a father and son to quest for men who've almost certainly died," Philip added, "all the while knowing they've missed their rescue boat?"

"Ship," Mansfield said.

Brillman laughed. "Sounds more like stupidity."

"There's a fine line between stupidity and faith," Petard said.

"If Pop hadn't been lucky enough to find this whaler," Kennedy said, "it *would* have been stupidity."

Jack shook his head. "There is no luck, Kennedy. There is only holding on long enough to outlast death."

Colin smiled and extended two fists. "Hail the conquering heroes, then."

"All hail!" Andrew shouted, putting his fists on his brother's.

The men drew a tight circle and instantly filled it with wiry arms and ragged sleeves. *"HAIL!"*

Kennedy shrugged. "Yeah, okay."

The fists gave way to open arms, and the men began embracing one another, vowing pledges and promises.

Lombardo was blubbering. "You saved my life. I don't know how I'll repay you all."

"Just show us it was worth the trouble," Kennedy remarked. "Get a job."

"I want every address," Ruskey said. "I'll write you all and send you prints."

"Lifetime free medical examinations for all of you and your families," Dr. Montfort offered. "Five-five-five Broadway, sixth floor."

"We'll all stay in touch," Hayes said. "Always. We're family."

"Brothers of the *Mystery*!" Cranston shouted. "Forever!"

Colin realized he loved them all. He believed the promises were sincere, and he felt a bond that would be painful to break.

But he suspected that after the landing, after contact with people, the return to routines and schedules and schooling, everything would change. All the promises and memories would gather in a dusty corner like a jewel too cumbersome to wear, only rarely to be brushed off and seen once again in vivid light.

As Colin turned back to the shore, he noticed four uniformed policemen around Mrs. Westfall, looking up sternly at the ship.

He glanced at Philip. "Are they waiting for you?"

"I figured something fishy was up with him," Talmadge remarked.

Philip nodded. "Yes. I robbed a bank. I took a flier on a stupid prank that went sour. That is why I was sent on this trip. My mother is Horace Putney's sister. She sent me to him to avoid prosecution. He, in turn, blackmailed your unsuspecting father into taking me on this trip."

"I knew all of that," Jack said.

"You *did?*" Philip asked.

"I pieced it together. And you know what? I'll be ever grateful to your uncle."

"You redeemed yourself in my eyes . . . deck rat," Captain Barth said with a smile.

"Why don't you just return the money, no hard feelin's?" Windham asked.

"I can't," Philip said. "It went down with the *Mystery.*"

"We can throw a block while you break for the open field," Ruppenthal suggested.

"No," Philip said firmly. "I couldn't hide from this in Antarctica. No civilized place will be easier. I will give myself up. What punishment could be worse than what I've just been through?"

"Listening to Lombardo sing?" Flummerfelt said.

"Having to look at Nigel every day," Kennedy chimed in. "Say, where is that two-legged warthog, anyway?"

Nigel was nowhere to be seen. "Probably in the fo'c'sle," Mansfield said, "flensing money from some poor underpaid whaler in a poker game."

As the *Nobadeer* was pulled into the dock's wood pilings, the dock workers rolled a sturdy, rope-railed gangplank to the hull. The dogs raced down first, followed by Kosta, grabbing tight to the railings and shouting, "*Prosecheh, paithàkia!*"

Philip was the next to step onto the plank. "Farewell," he said. "You are all cordially invited to my execution."

Colin followed him down, then Jack, Andrew, and Captain Barth. The other sailors nearly pushed themselves overboard trying to crowd onto the steps — all but Ruskey, who'd gone belowdecks to find his camera and film.

At the dock, Philip walked to his mother, who was now crying. He put his arms around her and held her for a long time, whispering into her ear, while the policemen kept a respectful distance.

Finally his mother said, "Philip, these are Constables Mudge, Lamston, and Pickering."

Mudge was well fed and self-satisfied, with a beard so thick it could hide a small pet. Lamston stood tall and erect, his nervous features twitching a well-waxed handlebar mustache that shone even in the fog. Pickering had a baby face, quizzical and amused, and his hat barely fit atop his thick blond locks.

Philip turned to them with his hands outstretched.

"No handcuffs at your age," said Constable Mudge. "We trust your mum. The other mums have been very helpful to us."

"Other mums?"

"Guess you 'aven't seen the newspapers," said Constable Lamston. "They pulled your pals by their ears into the police station. Photos made the front page. Not exactly seasoned criminals, you might say. Recovered all the money."

"Well, you can't recover my share," Philip said. "It's lost."

"We'll leave that matter to the magistrate," Mudge shot back. "'E'll 'ave some creative way to draw it out of your inheritance — or your wages, presumin' you ever earn any."

At the sudden sound of a scuffle aboard the *Nobadeer*, the officers looked upward. On deck, two rough-looking whalers were leading Nigel to Captain Coffin.

"'Ands off!" Nigel shouted. "I 'ave a perfickly good exclamation!"

"We found 'im 'idin' among the blubber barrels," one of the whalers said.

"Stowin' away — on a *whalin' ship?*" Coffin said. "Love ye the hunt so much?"

"My credentials is impregnable, I assure you," Nigel said. "Whales 'n' me, we go way back. I can sling me a harpool like the best of 'em — I mean it, Coffing, take me wif you — please!"

The policemen were grinning. "Well, well . . . what have we here?" murmured Pickering. "If it isn't Arnold Waxflatter."

"Arnold?" Philip repeated.

"*Waxflatter?*" Colin said.

"Goes under many names," Lamston said. "Wanted for shopliftin', bad credit, postal fraud, impersonatin' a sailor, impersonatin' just about anybody 'cept a law-abidin' cit'zen — not to mention cheatin' old widows and widowers by offerin' to invest their money and then disappearin' with it."

"That's our Nigel," Robert said.

"You," Mudge said to Philip, "is small potatoes compared to 'im."

Nigel — or Arnold — tried to hide his face as the whalers forced him down the gangplank. "Don't fink you'll get away wif this! I know my rights — this ship is neutrical jurisdinction, an' under international code I claim armistice!"

"Amnesty," Captain Barth corrected him.

"That, too!" Nigel said.

Lamston took Nigel roughly by the arm. "So, the *Nobadeer* goes out for a whale and comes back with a weasel."

"It's all a misunderstanding!" Nigel insisted. "I'm as innocent as the nap on a baby's cheek!"

"Save it for the courtroom," Lamston said.

Captain Barth stepped forward. "I can't speak as to the innocence or guilt of this man, but I will gladly testify as to the strength of his character."

Nigel's mouth dropped open. "You *will?*"

"He bagged a few whalefish single-'anded, eh?" Constable Pickering said.

"We are not whalers, sir," Jack said. "We were Antarctic explorers."

Mudge let out a guffaw. "And I'm the Archbishop of York."

"The Cap'n radioed us all about you," Lamston said. "Tol' us you was lost on a sloop somewhere off Cape 'orn."

"*What?*" Jack said.

"That's not true!" Colin exclaimed.

"It ain't?" Pickering said. "I suppose you reached the South Pole, too."

Mudge made a mockingly sad face. "Awww, 'at'll be a great disappointment to Captain Robert Falcon Scott. Too late to tell 'im now. 'E's somewhere between South Africa and New Zealand. Left 'ere on the first of June."

"Tell them, Captain Coffin!" Colin said.

Captain Coffin stepped roughly down the gangplank. "The boy has an active imagination. His team's too embarrassed to admit the truth, which is wha' I told you. It's human nature for Yankee rascals. Such as these ain't fit to eat off the shoes of a hero like Robert Scott. God save the King! Now where's that reward money ye promised, for me pickin' up yer bloody criminals 'n' deliverin' 'em to port?"

"You liar!" Andrew shouted.

"Coffin, you'll pay for this," Jack said.

"'S long's I collects me due first," Coffin replied.

The dock erupted with noise, every man of the *Mystery* shouting and advancing on Coffin.

With a grand sweep of his arm, Captain Coffin drew a polished sword. "Avast, ye rogues!"

Constable Mudge rolled his eyes. "My, if we ain't got Long John Silver in our midst."

"This is 1910, sir," Lamston announced. "Buckling swash in public is a criminal offense, punishable to the full extent of the law."

In the midst of the tumult, a gleaming, well-upholstered automobile purred to a stop just before the dock. The driver jumped out crisply and opened the passenger door.

Horace Putney swiveled his girth, grimacing as he surveyed the dock, and stepped out.

"Putney!" Father shouted. "Just in time."

"Good day, Uncle Horace, so *much* to tell you!" Philip called out. "But first, please inform these benighted souls where we have been!"

Putney strolled forward, ignoring Philip. He wore a full-length mink coat, and it swayed like a gentle brown sea over his exceedingly broad beam.

A fur hat of the Russian style sat like a nest on his head, and he puffed contentedly on a fat cigar. "Just where *have* you been?"

"In Antarctica, exactly as planned, Mr. Putney," Colin said.

"These scurvy bags o' bones says they reached the South Pole," Mudge exclaimed.

"We did not!" Andrew said. "But we tried."

"Mr. Putney financed the building of our barquentine, the *Mystery*," Colin said. "He sent supplies to us in Argentina. He'll vouch for us."

Putney raised his eyebrow. "Well, that's a mighty fine yarn, young fella. But I build houses, not boats. I see that my nephew picked his American friends true to form." He stole a wink at the policemen. "Carry on. I'll be along to the magistrate's to clear up this matter."

As the policemen escorted Philip away, he shouted, "Traitor!" over his shoulder. Captain Coffin followed behind, his flowing cape and clattering scabbard clearing the street.

Father was red. When he spoke, his words hissed through clenched teeth. "*Why*, Putney? Even for you this is despicable."

"I know why," Colin said, turning on Putney.

"You don't want to seem like a loser, do you? If we didn't reach the South Pole, then you're just another failure. You don't have the guts to admit the truth."

"What is the truth?" Putney asked.

"That you financed one of the bravest, most courageous expeditions ever made by Americans," Andrew replied.

"You didn't reach the Pole, did you?"

"No," Jack said. "We couldn't — we knew enough to cut our losses and turn back. But we reached closer than any American has. And we survived. That's a victory in itself."

"Jack, the world isn't looking for *closer*. They're looking for results, and now they have Robert Falcon Scott — a bona fide national hero — to hang their hopes on. You could have beaten him, but you didn't. Time moves on. I took a gamble on you and lost; my money's invested in Scott now." Putney shrugged. "I'm just doing what you did. Cutting my losses and moving on."

"We'll go to all the newspapers," Colin vowed. "We'll tell them what happened — and how you turned your back on us."

"Be my guests," Putney said. "See how many are interested, when they have a *real* race for the South Pole going on."

"Putney, you'll tell the truth someday," Jack said. "I won't stop hounding you until you do."

Putney chuckled. "Well, you'd be wise to book passage on two rather elaborate voyages, then. Tomorrow I leave on an around-the-world cruise. I arrive back in London in approximately a year and a half."

"We'll be right here, waiting," Jack replied.

"You'll wait a long time," Putney said, turning away. "Because shortly thereafter I'll be steaming back to New York on the most expensive and magnificent ocean liner in history."

The chauffeur opened the automobile door, and Putney stepped in, muttering impatiently, "To the magistrate at once! I'm running late."

As the motor started up again, Putney leaned out the window and waved.

"You'll find us in New York, Putney!" Colin shouted. "At the dock upon your return!"

"Very well," Putney called out, pulling away in a cloud of cigar smoke. "Look for the *Titanic*."

The Aftermath

A Postscript
(1910 to the Present)

Historical Notes on the Crew and the Legend

The story of the *Mystery* did not end in London.

All his life, Andrew Winslow corresponded with crew members and kept news clippings on those who led public lives. From these, and Andrew's unpublished journals, we know the following:

Captain Elias Barth continued commanding ships until he died, elderly and happy, in the port of Bermuda.

Kosta Kontonikolaos worked as a circus animal trainer/performer, and, like a modern-day Homer, told the *Mystery*'s saga to all who'd listen. Almost everyone understood it to be fiction, but a small cult of people, mostly kids, believed him — including Kosta's children and grandchildren, of whom there were many.

George Oppenheim began a slow recovery from a little-understood condition we now know as post-traumatic stress disorder. As a psychiatric social worker, he detected and treated the condition in countless soldiers returning from the First and Second World Wars. **Luis Rivera** worked as a longshoreman on the notoriously corrupt and violent New York City docks — and in the 1950s, on the verge of retirement, he helped lead the fight for unionization. **Robert,** as Robert Makela, prosperous importer of goods from Africa, marched on Selma with his four children in 1963 at age seventy-eight. He walked all the way.

Peter Mansfield, after years of sailing, published an archive of sea chanteys, now out of print. **David Ruskey** enjoyed great acclaim for his nature photography but always asserted his best work was left in a desolate Antarctic cove. Upon earning a doctorate of divinity, **Reverend Jacques Petard** led a thriving Lutheran parish in Chicago. **Pete Hayes** became a sixth-grade math teacher. Meteorologist **Harv Talmadge** helped the U.S. Weather Bureau recover its reputation a decade after it mispredicted the disastrous hurricane in Galveston, Texas. Starting with a Hoboken saloon, **Tim O'Malley** and **Rick Stimson** eventually established four popular Chez Tim et Richard restaurants in New Jersey — "Out-of-This-World Food, Down-to-Earth Prices." **Horst Flummerfelt,** foreseeing the mass popularity of the automobile, opened a booming garage and auto-parts store. **Chris Ruppenthal** and **Bruce Cranston** moved to Los Angeles and found success in the burgeoning talking-film industry. **Wyman Kennedy** worked his way from carpenter to building contractor, finally retiring to a cottage he built with his children on Squam Lake, New Hampshire. **Dr. Montfort** lived up to his promise of lifetime free medical care to crewmates. One patient was **Vincent Lombardo,** who, after retiring as a sailor, had a brief career in musical comedy, appearing most notably in *Mabel of the High Seas* on Broadway.

Most of the sailors saw action in the First World War, which was then called the Great War. Documents show that **James Windham** was killed in Arras, France, in 1917, and **Mike Sanders** died on the Western Front a year later.

Philip Westfall was released from police custody after Horace Putney's intervention. Upon receiving his inheritance at age eighteen, he was billed the entire amount of the stolen money, with interest, which he finally finished repaying at age thirty. He moved to a small but tastefully appointed cottage in the Cotswolds with his German shepherd, Schmetterling, and was never heard from again.

Arnold Waxflatter, also known as **Nigel,** was convicted on all counts and served a full ten-year sentence, repeatedly denied early release because of poor behavior. He settled in New York City, made a fortune in the stock market bull run of the 1920s, lost it all in the Crash of 1929, and was last seen selling health elixirs door-to-door in Arizona under the name Chet Farkas.

Information on other crew members is still being sought from friends and relatives.

Jack Winslow never sailed again. He enrolled at Columbia University at age forty-five and finished the undergraduate degree he'd begun at Harvard. He became friends with **Lawrence "Chappy" Walden** after a chance encounter while on vacation in Maine. Jack finally returned Walden's good luck gesture (with a piece of wood and grommeted rope from the *Mystery*, which Colin had saved) and eventually the two went into business, establishing the Northeastern Geological Survey Institute.

When he died at age eighty-three, in 1950, he considered himself a lucky man indeed.

For **Colin** and **Andrew Douglas Winslow,** the *Mystery* expedition was just the first of many adventures in a new century.

Colin was twenty-three when he served in the war. He lost the use of one arm because of an injury suffered while saving the life of a fellow soldier. Afterward, he stayed close to his father and brother in New York City, marrying and raising four burly sons, all of whom learned how to sail on Long Island Sound by the age of six.

Andrew followed his father's footsteps to Harvard but graduated with high honors. He was decorated for valor in the war for his work against German submarine attacks. Settling in Greenwich Village, he married, had a daughter, and lived a comfortably bohemian life as the author of a series of popular sea adventures. *Aurora Australis*, a thinly veiled account of the voyage of the *Mystery*, was his best-seller.

When the *Titanic* sank in 1912, **Horace Putney** jumped aboard a lifeboat, disguised as a woman. He perished while attempting to climb onto the rescue ship, slipping and falling back into the sea. He had never learned to swim.

He took the truth about the *Mystery* down with him.

The public did not pay much attention to the story about the ill-fated voyage. Ruskey searched the *Nobadeer* for his vest-pocket camera and film, but they were gone. Later Nigel admitted to hiding the equipment for himself among the blubber. Taking it for trash, the *Nobadeer* crew later dumped it in the sea somewhere off the coast of Martha's Vineyard. No photos survived.

In the absence of physical evidence, Jack Winslow sought out the shipbuilder, Samuel Breen, only to find that Breen had died of a heart attack shortly after the *Mystery* set sail. Breen's records were haphazard. They showed plans for the *Mystery*, but they gave Buenos Aires as its destination. Horace Putney still owed him more than half the money for the ship.

Breen's estate was never able to collect it.

The dockworkers in Buenos Aires confirmed the ship's arrival and departure, describing the crew as inept and badly organized. They fully believed that the ship could have been scuttled or capsized. For years after the expedition, the *Mystery*'s sailors tried to reveal their stories to the American press — and for a while a few reporters championed their cause. But after the shocking death of Robert Scott's party, Roald Amundsen's sensational and controversial conquering of the South Pole, followed by the amazing (and documented) survival sagas of Ernest Shackleton and Douglas Mawson, the press simply lost interest.

For years, the men of the *Mystery* met at convivial annual meetings that became less and less frequent. The last was held in Mansfield's home in Wayland, Massachusetts, in 1941, just before the United States entered the Second World War.

The plight of the *Mystery* remains a legend no more. But somewhere in this country a few Winslow great-grandchildren know the whole story.
And nothing stays secret forever.

Peter Lerangis
New York, New York
January 30, 2000

Glossary

abovedecks — any higher deck

adze — an axlike tool with a curved blade

amidships — in the center of the ship

aurora australis (also called *the southern lights*) — a mysterious formation of arcing lights in the Southern Hemisphere apparent most strongly in the Antarctic

avast — a nautical command that means Stop!

backwash — the backward movement of water as it is propelled behind an object

ballast — a heavy material (sometimes rocks) put at the bottom of a ship or boat to create stability

barnacle — a small crustacean with a pebblelike shell that attaches itself to rocks, boats, and ships

barque — a three- to five-masted sailing ship with all masts square-rigged except the aftermast, which is fore-and-aft rigged

barquentine — a three- to five-masted ship with a square-rigged foremast but fore-and-aft rigged mainmast and mizzenmast

batten (n) — a narrow wooden strip of wood

batten (v) — to fasten or secure with a batten

beam — the widest part of a ship

belowdecks — any lower deck

bilges — the lowest part of a boat or ship's inner hull

binnacle — a housing for a ship's compass

boom — the horizontal spar used to support the bottom edge of a sail

bow — the front of a ship

bowsprit — the spar extending from the bow of a ship

braces — a rope used to control horizontal movement of a square-rigged sail

brackish — salty

brash ice — ground-up ice floes and lumps of snow, with a puddinglike texture

breaker — a wave that breaks into foam

bulkhead — an upright partition that separates compartments of a ship

bulwarks — the side of a ship above the upper deck

calve — to break off a section of ice from a larger mass, as in an iceberg from an ice shelf

capsize — to overturn or to become overturned

cofferdam — a watertight structure to cover a hole in a ship's hull during repairs

come about — to change a ship's tack

crevasse — a deep crevice in ice or snow

crosstrees — the intersection of mast and horizontal spar in a square-rigged ship

crosswind — a wind that blows *across*, as opposed to *with* or *against*, a ship

Davy Jones's locker — the sea bottom

dead low — the absolute lowest point of the tide

deckhouse — a structure on the upper deck of a ship, which often contains officers' quarters

dinghy — a small boat, often carried on a larger boat or ship

doldrums — an area near the equator characterized by hot weather and a lack of wind

encroach — to advance more than the usual limits

exposure — a condition resulting from prolonged contact with severe weather; can result in death

feather (v) — to turn an oar, at the end of a stroke, so that its blade is horizontal as it pulls back above the water's surface, reducing wind resistance

flense — to strip blubber from a whale

flier, take a — to attempt a reckless act

fo'c'sle — abbreviation of *forecastle*, the area of a ship under the foresail of a ship; often where the sailors are housed

foremast — the mast at the bow end of a ship

furl (v) — to wrap a sail around something

greenheart — dark greenish wood, known for its durability, from a South American tree

grommet — a strong eyelet or loop, as on a sail, through which a rope is passed

growler — a small iceberg

gunwale — the highest edge of the ship's hull

guy line — a rope or wire connected between objects or people and used as a guide

gyre (n) — a circular movement; a giant circular current

halyard — a rope used to raise sails

hardtack — a hard, plain biscuit made of flour and water

heave to (past tense, hove to) — to turn a ship's bow into the wind and let the ship stay adrift in preparation for a storm

heel (v) — to lean to one side due to wind or waves

hoosh — stew

hull — the frame, or body, of a ship

hummock — a ridge of ice

hypothermia — a condition characterized by lower-than-normal body temperature

iceberg — a large mass of floating ice broken off (or *calved*) from shelf ice or from a glacier *ice floe* — a flat, floating fragment of sea ice

ice shelf (also shelf ice) — an ice sheet that begins on land and extends into the water, resting on the sea bottom

jibe — to move sails from one side to the other while sailing into the wind, in order to change the ship's direction

jury-rigged — put together in a makeshift fashion

keel — the central timber at the bottom of the ship, running from bow to stern

lash — to bind with a rope

lay (n) — a share of profit paid instead of wages

lay to — to bring a ship to a stop in open water, facing the wind

lead (n) — a path of water through pack ice

lee — the side sheltered from the wind

maelstrom — a turbulent, powerful whirlpool

mainmast — the second mast from the bow after foremast (middle mast on the *Mystery*)

mainsail — the bottom sail on the mainmast

mast — the vertical pole that supports sails

Melville, Herman (1819–1891) — American novelist who wrote *Moby-Dick*

mizzenmast (or *mizzen*) — the sail on the aft end of a ship (the third sail on the *Mystery*)

Nansen, Fridtjof (1861–1930) — famous Norwegian Arctic explorer

oarlock — a metal U-shaped device that keeps an oar in place

old ice — ice floes that have remained unmelted from previous seasons, usually dense and hummocky

pemmican — food made from dried meat and filler such as flour, molasses, or dried fruit

port — the left side of a ship (as you face bow)

pressure — the force exerted by two ice floes pushing against each other

pressure ridge — ice that has been pushed upward between colliding ice floes

Primus stove — a small, portable metal stove consisting of one burner and a wire platform over it

prow — see *bow*

pudding ice — see *brash ice*

put in — to enter a port, cove, or harbor

put to — to head for shore

reel (n) — a spirited Scottish Highlands dance

rigging — an arrangement of sails, spars, and ropes

riptide — a strong crosscurrent caused by the action of water against a shore or edge of an ice floe

rudder — a plate mounted at the ship's stern for directing its course, turned by means of a *tiller*

runner — either of two long, thin, parallel tracks of wood attached to the bottom of a vehicle, on which it moves through snow

scuttle — to sink a ship by means of a hole in the hull

sheet — a rope attached to the bottom of a sail, used to change the angle of the sail relative to the wind

ship water (v) — to take in water over the ship's hull

sledge — a sled used for transporting loads over the ice

sloop — a boat with one fore- and aft-rigged mast and one staysail

southern lights — see *aurora australis*

spar — a pole that supports sails and rigging

spindrift — a sea spray blown by the wind

square-rigged — an arrangement of square- or rectangular-shaped sails

starboard — the right side of a ship (as you face bow)

stave in (past tense, stove in) — to smash or crush inward

staysail — a triangular sail supported by a *stay*, or diagonal halyard, as opposed to a mast

stern — the rear of a ship

stream ice — pack ice that contains leads

tack — to change the direction of a ship, usually by turning the bow into the wind *taffrail* — the rail at the stern of the ship

tailwind — a wind roughly in the same direction as the ship's motion (a wind blowing from *behind*)

tarpaulin — a waterproof canvas covering

tiller — a lever with which to turn a rudder and steer a boat

trace(s) — a strap(s) connecting a harnessed dog to a sledge

trim — to arrange sails for the optimal speed and direction

unstep — to remove (a mast)

waterline — the line made by the surface of the water against a ship's hull

water sky — a dark streak on the horizon that indicates open ocean

whirlpool — a circular current of water (see *maelstrom*)

winch — a machine containing a drum around which is curled a rope or wire for pulling or lifting

yaw (v) — to move erratically off course

yeti — the legendary snow beast of Nepal; came to be known as the abominable snowman, Sasquatch, or Bigfoot

Bibliography

Alexander, Caroline. *Endurance: Shackleton's Legendary Antarctic Expedition*. Alfred A. Knopf, 1999. Includes excellent reproductions of Antarctic photos taken by master polar photographer Frank Hurley.

Armstrong, Jennifer. *Shipwreck at the Bottom of the World: Shackleton's Amazing Voyage*. Crown Publishers, 1998.

Bickel, Leonard. *Mawson's Will*. Avon Books, 1977. Thrilling survival story; Douglas Mawson walked 320 miles across Antarctica after a companion and all his dogs and equipment fell into a crevasse.

Cherry-Garrard, Apsley. *The Worst Journey in the World*. Carroll & Graf, 1989. Robert Falcon Scott's fatal voyage to the South Pole.

Huntford, Roland. *Scott & Amundsen*. G. P. Putnam's Sons, 1980. The race between Scott and Amundsen for the South Pole, with photos and maps.

Lansing, Alfred. *Endurance: Shackleton's Incredible Voyage*, Carroll & Graf, 1986. The most exciting account of the Shackleton expedition.

Maloney, Elbert S. *Chapman Piloting*. Hearst Marine Books (various ed.). Good book for basic sailing information.

Shackleton, Ernest. *South*. Carroll & Graf, 1998. A memoir of the voyage of the *Endurance* by its legendary leader. Full of interesting details.

Worsley, F. A. *Shackleton's Boat Journey*. W. W. Norton & Company, 1977. Written by the captain of the *Endurance*, an account of what many call the greatest boat journey in the world, by Shackleton, Worsley, and four other men, across the Drake Passage on a modified 22-foot lifeboat.

Websites:

www.terraquest.com/antarctica/index.html. Excellent introduction to Antarctica; good photos.

www.ista.co.uk.com. Diagrams and terminology for various sailing ships and rigs.

www.theice.org. Facts and figures about Antarctica.

www.pbs.org/wgbh/nova/shackleton. Excellent web documentary of Shackleton's fabled transantarctic voyage, contemporary adventures, and lots of good general information about Antarctica. Video clips.

www.acronet.net/~robokopp/shantys.html and www. woodenshipsmusic.com/links.html. Information and sound clips about sea chanteys.

Working seaports and seaport museums in the U.S.A.:

Mystic Seaport, P.O. Box 6000, 75 Greenmanville Avenue, Mystic, CT 06355-0990 (Visitor Information 860-572-5315, toll free 1-888-SEA-PORT), http://www.mysticseaport.org/

South Street Seaport Museum, 207 Front Street, New York, NY 10038 (212-748-8600), http://www. southstseaport.org/

Texas Seaport Museum, Pier 21 and Harborside Drive, Galveston, TX 77550 (409-763-1877, fax 409-763-3037), http://www.phoenix.net/~tsm/

Independence Seaport Museum, 211 S. Columbus Boulevard, Philadelphia, PA 19106 (215-413-8621), http://www.libertynet.org/seaport/

Acknowledgments

I began researching this book while waiting long hours to be selected as a juror, so my first thanks go to the New York City criminal court system. Anne Fadiman, my good friend and an avid Antarctica buff, provided great enthusiasm and much research material from her amazing personal library. The real Peter Mansfield, whom I've had the good fortune of knowing for twenty-five years, helped enormously with nautical terminology. I thank the real Larry Walden for his patient tutelage during several summer afternoons sailing on Casco Bay, and his thorough evaluation of this book for sailing authenticity. And my mother, Mary Lerangis, who sent me to Greek school when I was a kid and shouldn't have had to correct all my Greek language mistakes, nevertheless did so with great joy. *Efharistò, s' aghapò.*

About the Author

Peter Lerangis is the author of *Antarctica: Journey to the Pole* and of the award-winning sci-fi/mystery series *Watchers*, the first book of which earned a 1999 Quick Pick for Young Adult Reluctant Readers award. His classic YA thrillers, *The Yearbook* and *Driver's Dead*, have been enjoyed in this country and throughout the world. His recent movie adaptations include *The Sixth Sense*, *El Dorado*, and *Sleepy Hollow*. Peter is a Harvard graduate with a degree in biochemistry and experience as a Broadway actor, which he feels are eminent qualifications for writing fiction. He lives in New York City with his wife, Tina deVaron, and their two sons, Nick and Joe. Peter is the eldest child of Nicholas Lerangis and the former Mary Kontonikolaos.